The Divine Wind
A Love Story

The Divine Wind
A Love Story

BY GARRY DISHER

Arthur A. Levine Books
AN IMPRINT OF SCHOLASTIC PRESS

Library of Congress Cataloging-in-Publication Data
Disher, Garry.

  The Divine Wind: A Love Story / by Garry Disher

    p. cm.

  Summary: On the eve of World War II, Hart, an Australian boy and
  Mitsy, a Japanese-Australian girl, fall in love but are driven apart.

  ISBN 0-439-36915-0

  1. World War, 1939–1945 — Australia — Juvenile fiction. [1. World
War, 1939–1945 — Australia — Fiction. 2. Interpersonal relations — Fiction.
3. Japanese — Australia — Fiction. 4. Australia — History — 20th century — Fiction.]
I. Title.

  PZ7.D6228 Di 2002

  [Fic] — dc21   2001038645

10 9 8 7 6 5 4 3 2   03 04 05 06

Printed in the United States of America
First American edition, May 2002

To Nancy Jerrick

Prologue
1946

In the final weeks of 1941, when I was adrift in life and my sister was missing in a war zone, my father offered our home as sanctuary to a young Japanese woman named Mitsy Sennosuke, unaware that I was in love with her. This was in Broome, in the northwest of Australia, at the time of the invasion of Malaya, when Japanese bombs were falling like silver rain and old certainties were crumbling, when some who had been our friends were now treated as aliens, transfigured by enmity and fear.

My father, Michael Penrose, was a pearling master. He ran a fleet of six pearling luggers, crewed by Malays, Manilamen, and Koepangers, with one Japanese diver on each lugger, and owned Penrose Chandlery Supplies, an airy tin-and-flywire shop situated at the head of the jetty that juts into Roebuck Bay.

We lived at the southern end of Broome, where many of the master pearlers lived. Broome was a straggling mile of wood and corrugated-iron shops and dwellings, and our house was a typical timber and iron bungalow on stilts, with broad verandas on all sides, shuttered windows, and a kitchen separate from the rest of the house. Creepers choked the verandas. Houses like ours were built to capture the cool morning and evening sea winds. The sun always beat down, but it reached us — on the veranda or in one of the rooms — as gauzy light through the creepers or banded through the shutters. We enjoyed our tropical existence: mangoes and barramundi on the table, bamboo furniture, sièstas, sundowners, pearlshell ashtrays, servants.

But together with the cheerful clamor, an atmosphere of faint pain surrounded our house. My father had preserved my mother's name upon the bow and stern of his leading lugger, the *Ida Penrose,* but the love that had inspired it was increasingly under strain in my teenage years, as my mother grew to hate Broome in all of its moods and almost, almost, to hate Alice, my father, and me.

She was from England, originally, and had been governess to some inland children when my father met her. You could say that, unlike the rest of us, she did not have red dirt, mangroves, or pearls in her blood.

I want to be fair to my mother. She loved Alice and me, and, for a long time, loved my father. It's even possible that she continued to love my father after she left us and returned to England to be with her elderly mother, but that's something I'll never know. But I do know that she wanted the best for us.

It could not have been easy for her. We were too careless, too casual, too democratic for her tastes. Our lives revolved around the seasons and the sea. There were two seasons — the Wet, from November to March, when the northwest was subject to cyclones; and the Dry, when the waters were safe again. During the long months of the Wet, my father would grumble about in his shop, undertake pointless maintenance of his luggers, which were laid up along the Dampier Creek mudflats, or bicker at home with my mother. He'd meddle in the garden and itch to be more useful than he was. Then, blessedly, the skies would clear and his mood would lift, and he'd put to sea again in the *Ida Penrose,* leading his little fleet to the pearling grounds. But sometimes he'd not return for weeks at a time, and that worried my mother.

So she chafed. She wanted coolness, calmness, greenness. She wanted England. She filled the house with Dickens,

Austen, Keats, the Brontë sisters, and we read them to please her, but were too restless and unused to reflection to talk to her about our reading, and my father and I preferred travelers' tales of remote Australia — books about ourselves, in other words — which left her cold. She'd push *Great Expectations* into our hands, and we'd say, "Too thick, I'll never get through it."

The garden was symptomatic of her alienation. It consisted of a lawn divided by white shellgrit paths, a scattering of coconut, fan, and traveler palms, and poincianas, frangipani, and bougainvillea, all of it severely groomed, but attractive to corellas and yellow-necked lorikeets. Over the years my father had dragged home old lugger anchors, diving helmets, and huge stone jars, and stationed them like so much statuary among the trees. Where my mother wanted the sort of profusion that can be found in an English garden, where she could have wandered and mused and loaded her arms with cuttings whenever she wanted, she got my father's bizarre mix of orderliness, rust, and verdigris. She'd wanted a gentleman, and got a man who gave off a sea-wrack sense of sweat and humble, dirty hands.

He said to her once accusingly, "Ida, you want me to be a veranda pearler."

She dabbed at the perspiration on her brow with a

scented linen handkerchief. "Michael, I want you home, I want you safe."

My father was scornful of veranda pearlers. They were men who, in prosperous times, wore white duck suits, white buckskin shoes, and pith helmets, and who, even when times were bad, never put to sea.

"You want me to play tennis with the magistrate and bridge with the bank manager and get us invited to dinner parties," my father said.

Stiff, uncomfortable, reproving, my mother left the room. In the silence that followed, my father rolled a cigarette, stuck it in the corner of his mouth, and said to Alice and me, in his winking, chiacking, kidding way, "Poor old Mum, she'd like to live in a big house, somewhere cool, with lots of servants."

Alice pushed back her chair. "That's not true. That's not fair."

My father tried to laugh it off. "Well, you know . . ."

I left the room with Alice. Our relationship with our mother was often awkward, but we didn't like to take sides. We knew that Ida wanted only to feel less at odds with the world in which she'd found herself. She had no one to talk to, no one listened, and so, in her loneliness and frustration, she seemed to develop the snobberies and prejudices of a colonial wife in the tropics.

It's hardly surprising, then, that she recoiled from the racial mix of Broome. She hated it when Alice and I spent time with Bin Mahomet, Lefinas Maloki, and Simeon Espada, the deckhands on the *Ida Penrose*. I don't recall that she ever wandered into Chinatown. And she certainly didn't approve of our friendship with the Sennosuke family. She didn't trust them. She suspected them of strange practices. She'd have said, dismissively, "Oh, don't be silly, Hart," if I'd admitted to being in love with Mitsy Sennosuke.

But she did understand love itself. She did understand what it is to love someone different from yourself. She understood what it is to wait for something to change, just as I'm waiting now, waiting for Mitsy to come back to me.

Trade Winds

In the Register of Aliens the Sennosukes were listed as Imazaki, Sadako, and Mitsu, but those names were too foreign to our ears, and so Imazaki was soon corrupted to "Zeke" and "Mitsu" to Mitsy — although Sadako, Mitsy's mother, was only called Sadako, for some reason.

Zeke was my father's diver on board the *Ida Penrose*. He was a slim, fit, sun-browned man, who wore his hair scraped back tight over his scalp. This gave him a strangely ascetic appearance, one at odds with the many scars and pebbly knocks he'd accumulated from shipwrecks and diving mishaps over the years.

It was said that Sadako had been smuggled into Broome

in a secret compartment in the hull of a Japanese mail boat in 1901, and sent to work in a brothel, where Zeke met her. I know that such things happened, but, in a place like Broome, nobody much cared. Unless conditions in the internment camp have altered her, Sadako is still a small, slightly rounded, and mostly silent woman with downcast eyes. I never saw her dressed in anything but a kimono. Before it all went wrong, she was famous for her soy sauce, which she manufactured in a tiny tin-shed factory in Chinatown. She also worked in our chandlery shop one day a week, speaking just enough English to sell rope, cleats, tar, sailcloth, and charts to fishermen and pearling men.

Mitsy represented a new generation. Born and educated in Broome, she slipped easily from speaking Japanese in John Chi Lane to speaking English with Alice and me. The three of us went everywhere together. My mother didn't approve, but Mitsy was Alice's best friend, and given that Alice is only a year younger than me, Mitsy became my friend too. I suppose it was Mitsy's *Japaneseness* that my mother feared, but the Mitsy we knew was composed of twin natures: retiring and modest with her parents and other Japanese families, and raucous and tireless with everyone else.

My memory tells me that Mitsy was beautiful. In fact, she had uneven features on a narrow head, which gave her face a permanently skeptical cast, as though she never fully believed the things she witnessed. Her bottom lip stuck out. Her hair was not fine and straight but thick and dryish, and in need of constant attention. Hers was a face of secret knowledge and good humor rather than classical beauty, but I am reading beauty and loveliness into it now because Mitsy saved me from myself and for a time we were very close.

The Sennosukes lived in Chinatown, in three rooms at the rear of a galvanized-iron boardinghouse in John Chi Lane, where double-storied dwellings breathed over one another across a gap no wider than a small car, and music leaked scratchily from tiny rooms lit by oil lamps. To get to it, Alice and I liked to take a long route through Chinatown, attracted by the Chinese gamblers, the Japanese divers, the lemon-squash stallholder, the Amboinese woman stirring mangrove crabs in a spitting wok, the sly-grog sellers, the half-dozen languages, and the slap of sandals and bare feet. Then one sharp double-knock on Mitsy's door, and Sadako would shout, "You Hartley Alice, you come in now."

Through the door, into a short, narrow passageway. The door on the left led to a sitting room, furnished with cast-off armchairs and a large steamer trunk with a batik cloth over it. The door on the right led to the bedroom: Zeke's and Sadako's double bed, and, in the corner, separated from it by a rice-paper screen, Mitsy's single bed and her bookcase. At the rear was a tiny kitchen and a lean-to bathroom.

Mitsy wasn't ashamed of where she lived, or ashamed of her parents, but she always bundled us out quickly. Her place was simply too small to contain us all, and the noise from boardinghouse tenants in tiny rooms on all sides was too distracting. Besides, we loved to wander.

Like most children in a town full of exotic distractions, we were invisible and highly mobile, three scrappy, swivel-necking kids, restlessly pulling in sensations. Red dirt roads scribbled through gray scrubland at the edge of Broome, the flat blue sea glittered or tossed green in the wind, and water sucked unseen in the mangrove belts. At low tide, soldier crabs marched on the mudflats, and water pools stared glassily up at the sun. We'd tramp to the end of the jetty, or ride the little steam train that carried goods and people the half-mile between the beach and the Singapore to Fremantle steamer whenever it berthed at the pier head.

We'd linger at the foreshore camps, where sailmakers and carpenters worked and elderly Malay fishermen unloaded dinghy loads of fish from the traps before stringing them along water-softened oars, to be shouldered up to the hotels. On the rocks below Cable Beach, men too old for pearling would fill white enamel billy cans with cockle oysters. Men like these were as shifty as gypsies to my mother, the way they came to the back door, hawking their oysters or suggesting that if she had a shilling to spare they would rehang the tilting shutter.

Then we'd head down to Ganthaume Point to touch the striated, wind-sculpted sandstone walls, and finally walk back along a gravel road newly cleared of bottles and tins by a chain gang from the jail.

That's what I remember most clearly, the good times, the balmy days of the Dry, when the trade winds blew, the sky was hung with stars at night, and Broome slumbered, waiting for the Wet, when the pearling fleets would return to port and lay up for the next few months. The fuels that drove us were curiosity and the need to escape the house, stories and the nearby sea, and the many scents of Broome: saltwater tides and mock-orange blossom, incense and burning dung, cotton heated by the sun, spices in hot oil.

•

I fell in love with Mitsy in the darkness of the tin-walled cinema in Sheba Lane, where cowboys roamed the range and airmen spies slipped away from foreign countries in the light of the moon, and great white hunters saved beautiful women from maddened rogue elephants.

In the daylight, Mitsy was a separate being, slim and restless and full of jokes and mischief, like Alice, but when the lights were dimmed and the screen glowed with lovers and heroes, she would grow quiet and still, and settle in her seat, and imperceptibly shift until her shoulder and knee touched mine. Alice, on the other side of her, would crane her head around and meet my gaze, but never say anything, or tease, just as Mitsy would never acknowledge the intimacy when the lights came on at the end but simply treat me as one of the gang again. I sometimes thought that I dreamed her.

Afterward we'd pile out into the odors and sounds of Chinatown and wander, Alice and Mitsy discussing the film intently, half turned to each other and bumping shoulders as they gestured and joked and reenacted the love scenes that, only minutes before, had so absorbed Mitsy. I would trail behind, feeling a little cut off from them.

But once, I remember, Mitsy turned and stared at me with a look of such solemn concentration, as though deciding something about me, that I reached out my hand and said, "Mitsy?"

Her expression cleared. She laughed, shoved Alice off the footpath, and said, "Race you to the jetty."

•

The cinema, the jetty, the beach, Chinatown, the Dampier Creek mudflats, that's where you'd find us out of school hours — not at Mitsy's house, certainly not at ours.

It wasn't only that our mother was cool and distant if Alice and I did bring Mitsy home with us, it was the worsening atmosphere there. We didn't want Mitsy to know about our troubles.

By the time I was fifteen, Ida had virtually stopped talking to my father. She'd be gentle and distracted with Alice and me, but shut down whenever my father was in the room. She'd also begun to disappear for hours at a time. We'd never see her leave the house, but she'd return late in the afternoon, looking rested and peaceful, almost dazed, before we broke into her dreams again.

"Do you know where she goes?" my father would ask us. "Bugger if I know."

As it happened, my mother's stiffness, distance, and exaggerated calm finally broke on a day when Mitsy was there to see it.

Fine and Flashing

We were not alone in having servants. Most European households employed at least a gardener and a house girl.

Saltwater Jack and his wife, Bernadette, lived in a room built onto the laundry at the rear of our house. Jack had been born on an island in Torres Strait and lured by force or slippery promises to work the luggers as a pearlshell opener when he was twelve. He was in his thirties before the war, but looked seventy, a man stooped and bent at angles by poorly knitted bone breaks.

Bernadette cleaned for my mother. She'd been separated from her family when she was little and raised and educated at the Broome convent school, where the nuns told her that she was born in sin of a Malay mother and an Aboriginal father, and would never amount to more than being a servant for someone like my mother.

A few years before the events of this story, Bernadette's brother had tracked her down. His name was Derby Boxer and he'd been raised on a Pallotine Catholic mission. When he was thirteen he had run away from the mission to find his father's people, tribal blacks on Hartog Downs, a sheep and cattle station on the coast south of Broome. Derby didn't stay long. He was so struck by the horsemanship of the stockmen on Hartog Downs that he left the camps of his people and asked Carl Venning, the station owner, for a job.

Eventually he was promoted to head stockman. This earned him certain privileges, including his own living quarters and regular trips to Broome with Venning. It was on one of these trips that he found Bernadette. She was the only one left of his immediate family, and he hadn't seen her since he was five.

After making contact, Derby became a regular visitor to our house, bedding down on a mattress in the laundry whenever Venning stayed in town on station business. Derby always looked fine and flashing, dressed in a clean, pressed, sun-bleached shirt and trousers, highly polished boots, and a broad-brimmed black hat. Silver gleamed on his belt and he liked to tie a red kerchief at his throat. I wasn't surprised to see him in the tin cinema in Sheba Lane, watching cowboy films.

Meanwhile Alice had begun to take notice of Carl Venning whenever he dropped Derby off. Venning was in his midtwenties then, ten years older than Alice, and charming in a reckless, knockabout way. I didn't like him, and nor did my mother, but he managed to charm Alice and my father.

I'd tease Alice: "Who's that old codger dropping Derby off? Looks like someone's grandfather. No, my mistake, it's Carl Venning."

And she'd smile sweetly: "Poor little boy, you'll grow up to be a real man one day."

We didn't know it until later, but Derby was a drinker. After the strain of mustering sheep and cattle and managing stockmen six days a week, he liked to unwind in Broome with cowboy films and cheap wine. Saltwater Jack and Bernadette didn't drink, and didn't approve of his drinking, and we all knew that my mother would hate it, so a conspiracy developed between us to hide his drinking from her.

Derby wasn't an ugly or a vicious drunk. More often than not he'd simply slide into a deep sleep, but along the way he tended to sing and giggle, or grow affectionate and sentimental. Saltwater Jack would attract our attention when Ida's back was turned, and we'd slip out and help him smuggle Derby around the side of the house and into the laundry. Sometimes my father would have to drive off in our Nash and collect Derby from some alley or creek bank.

One Saturday afternoon, Alice, Mitsy, and I went to see a pirate film. On Saturdays the cinema showed one film after another. You could come and go as you liked, and so there were already people in some of the seats. Mitsy touched my hand: "Isn't that Derby?"

It was, slumped awkwardly in the middle of one of the front rows, which had been set aside unofficially for Aborigines and Islanders.

"Is he all right?"

"He's fine," I assured her.

We settled into our seats. The lights dimmed. Then, in perfect synchronization, Mitsy and I sighed and our arms and knees touched. The screen flickered. A pirate swung from a rope, a cutlass in his teeth. Later there was a kiss. Mitsy pressed her knee against mine.

A hard, sudden snore, as sharp as the tearing of a cotton sheet. Then another. Some people murmured, others sniggered. It went on. There were angry shouts. "Shut up," and "Throw him out," and "Put a cork in it."

Mitsy whispered. "It's Derby. We should do something."

She sounded upset. I leaned closer and replied, "He's only sleeping it off. Let him be."

She shook her head violently. "People are laughing. Someone might hurt him. We should do something."

Alice peered around her. "She's right, Hart."

I got up with them but in bad grace. I was sulking, and didn't care if Mitsy saw it. I wanted her to know that I was disappointed, that I wanted to stay resting against her in the darkness. Instead, she was disappointed in me. I noticed her frown and turn away.

We edged out of our row and reached Derby just as the usher was prodding him with the butt of a torch. He recoiled. "This man's drunk."

"We'll take care of it," Alice said.

The light from the screen was very bright. The usher glanced at us distastefully. I thought I knew what he was thinking. What were two white kids doing with a Japanese kid? What were the three of them doing with a drunken Aborigine?

"Take him outside if he's yours," the man said. "At once, if you don't mind."

"Get stuffed," Mitsy said.

Alice giggled.

With Alice on one side of Derby and me on the other, and Mitsy behind him if he should fall, we carried Derby out onto the footpath. "Now what?"

"We take him home," Mitsy said.

The afternoon was ruined. I groaned and said sharply, "Come on then, let's get it over with."

Our lurching progress through the town woke Derby and soon he was walking unaided. He looked ashamed. "This fella orright now. You kids go."

"We'll see you home," Mitsy said.

We didn't make it. *"What on earth?"*

It was my mother, returning from somewhere, a book in one hand, a pair of fawn gloves in the other. She wore a hat to shade her from the sun and carried a clutch bag under her arm. She looked too fine for the streets of Broome, a beautiful woman who should never have left London. Where had she been? Where did she go when she left the house? I thought these things even as I sensed that meeting her like this was fatal.

"Hartley," she said. "Alice. What on earth is going on?"

She scarcely glanced at Mitsy or Derby.

"We were just —"

Derby chose that moment to step in front of her and remove his hat and beam crookedly. "These here good kids, missus. Help this ol' blackfella —"

My mother froze. "You're drunk."

"Only little bit, missus."

She ignored him. "What are you children doing with him?"

Mitsy said firmly, "We're taking him back to your place, Mrs. Penrose."

My mother regarded her for a moment. "I think it's time you went home, don't you?"

I saw bewilderment and hurt and then a dark scowl pass across Mitsy's face. She turned from my mother and stared at me. I jerked my head as a way of saying, Go, we'll catch up with you later, but Mitsy misinterpreted it, thinking that I was dismissing her too. She blinked uncomprehendingly at me, then her expression hardened and she spun around on her heel and fled.

Alice stormed at my mother: "That wasn't necessary."

"Oh, I think it was, Alice."

"I hate you."

And Alice fled, calling, "Mitsy! Wait!"

My mother sighed. "Hart, I want an explanation."

I stared miserably at the ground. "We were helping Derby back to Jack and Bernadette's."

"Look at me, please. This is not the first time Derby's had too much to drink, is it."

"No."

My mother nodded. After a while she turned to Derby. She was very gentle. "I'm sorry, Mr. Boxer, but in the circumstances I think it best if you find somewhere else to stay when you're in Broome."

"Orright, missus."

Quest for Paradise

You could say that this is a story about friendship, and the betrayal of friendship, and friendships lost and regained.

Friendship is a slippery notion. We lose friends as we change and our friends don't, or as we form other alliances, or as we betray our friends or are ourselves betrayed. We often *make* friends for the weakest of reasons — proximity, for example, or shared experience, or laziness or need — but what will make them endure as friends? Their similarity to us? Their utter difference from us?

I knew only that I'd lost Mitsy's friendship. Alice hadn't — she sided with Mitsy. It didn't mean that I never spent time with them, but things had changed. If we went to the cinema, Mitsy sat on one side of Alice, I on the other. Out in the street, she was polite but distant with me.

Things changed further when, shortly after the incident with Derby and my mother, I finished my last year of school and went to work with my father. It was 1938 and Alice and Mitsy had one more year to go. Now I saw less and less of them. I felt friendless, in need of a friend.

Then one day Jamie Kilian came into the chandlery shop. He'd been in Broome since the end of the Wet, and I'd seen him about, looking standoffish and difficult, as if to make the point that no one would be doing *him* any favors, and so I'd never bothered to introduce myself. His manner seemed to say: I'm new, a city kid who's been landed in this rough-edged northern town far from anywhere simply because my father's been appointed to a government job here, but that doesn't mean I need friends.

He began to stroll about the shop, picking things up and putting them down again. I watched him. Jamie had dark, hard, searching eyes. He was shorter than me, tough and nuggety looking, with wiry black hair.

I said, "Can I help you?"

"Just looking."

I watched him walk about the shop and stop at a glass case of seafaring artifacts that my father had installed in one corner. "That's old."

It was a pocket watch. "One of my father's divers found it on the seabed. Eighteenth century."

After a while he told me his name. We shook hands awkwardly, and I found myself saying, "Would you like to come to a birthday party?"

He faced me suspiciously, as if I'd asked a trick question. His father was the new magistrate, and magistrates, like policemen, deal mostly with people who have something to hide. "Whose party?"

"Mine."

He relaxed a little, narrowed his hard eyes, and tilted his solid head. "How old?"

"Seventeen."

The expression that passed across his face was secretive and quick, but I could see that my answer had pleased him in some way. I later learned that he was older than me by almost ten months. He liked having that edge over me. Jamie was competitive. In almost everything you could name, Jamie was better than me, and so we became friends, for it kept him on top. We were also opposites. Where I idled abstractedly, full of useless longings and dreams, Jamie snapped into action. Where my eyes were lost on far horizons, Jamie kept his fixed firmly on what was in front of him. Where I was tall, graceful, and lazy, Jamie Kilian was compact, restless, and alert. My hair flopped over my eyes, leached of color by the sun, but Jamie's was tight, waxy, and controlled. I was given to complicated moods and introspection, but Jamie embraced life, almost smacking his hands together in satisfaction at what it might bring him.

But it was I who made the first move. I offered friendship before he did.

"Where and when?" he asked.

I told him about my father and his fleet of luggers, and how we'd be celebrating on board the *Ida Penrose*. Jamie's eyes gleamed a little. I had offered him a whiff of the sea and seafaring, so I suppose you could say that I was exotic to him and not just someone he could throw into the shade.

•

It was a difficult, frustrating birthday party. There were too many kids, and with my father acting the goat, trying to amuse us, and Mitsy standing apart from everything, her arms folded, I was too distracted to enjoy myself. I saw very little of Jamie. He seemed to spend most of his time talking to Ida, who appeared for the first hour, and then to Alice.

But at one point I saw him leaning on the stern rail with Mitsy. I made my way past the wheelhouse to join them.

Jamie sprang back from the rail. "The birthday boy," he said. His face was flushed. He was grinning.

I rested my forearms on the rail and tried to meet Mitsy's gaze. "Hello."

She didn't respond. The only words she'd said were "Happy birthday," when she'd first come aboard with Zeke and Sadako.

Jamie said, "I've been meeting your family and your friends."

"So I see."

Something in my tone and the attitude of my body alerted Jamie to the hidden currents in my life. He straightened, looked at me, looked at Mitsy, and I saw his eyes gleam in understanding.

He seemed to push it a little, twisting the blade. "You didn't tell me about Mitsy, Hart. What a corker!"

He grinned disarmingly at her as he said it. She looked down shyly, murmured something, and slipped away.

"Sorry, did I say something wrong? Put my big foot in it?"

"Forget it," I said.

Then my father appeared, rubbing his hands together. "No lurking about, you two. Time for charades."

•

One outcome of that party was that my mother invited the Kilians to dinner. "She thinks it'll improve our standing in the community," my father said later. He continued to be hurt and bewildered by her solitariness.

Broome was a town full of government servants. We had teachers, troopers, clerks, inspectors. We had the postmaster, the customs agent, the hospital superintendent, the harbormaster.

And we had Jamie Kilian's father. Like his son, Magistrate Kilian was restless and inquiring. An older-looking version of Jamie — short, dark, solid — he seemed to start walling us in with words as soon as he'd ushered his wife and son ahead of him through our front door. As the locals put it later, the bugger sure could talk.

All through dinner, he lectured us. "Here, in the north, is the real Australia."

My father looked at him doubtfully. "Is it?"

"The cities down south? Soft and complacent. This is where the future lies."

"Does it?"

"Mark my words. Populate or perish. More people, closer settlement, that's the answer, not the pastoral industry. The cattlemen are holding us back."

"You could have a point."

"My word I do. If we were to break up the big pastoral leases and allow farmers to develop the soil for agriculture, on lots of smaller leases, we'd soon have new towns up here, with work for fencers, stockmen, carpenters, roadmakers, storekeepers, builders, and civil servants. Eventually the part-Aboriginal will die out. The tribal blackfellow can be left in his native state."

I glanced at Jamie. He was sitting very stiffly, staring hard at the wall, as if he wanted to be somewhere else. I wondered what disappointments drove him.

I glanced at Alice. She was scowling at her plate. Given that she was fond of Carl Venning, a pastoralist, she'd hardly welcome criticism of his way of life from a know-all like Jamie Kilian's father.

Meanwhile Mr. Kilian was warming to his theme. He seemed to be saying that we had the potential to enact a racial experiment in the north, and breed a superior Australian type. "The bush represents purity. We can make it a paradise if we select the right kind of people to settle and have families here."

Jamie's mother cleared her throat. "You're browbeating your hosts, dear."

She had the tired, tentative look of a woman who'd been ignored all her married life, who had no expectations, and I was not surprised when her husband cut her off with a careless flick of his hand. "Good English stock," he continued, "not your Continental rubbish."

I didn't care one way or the other, but I said, to stir him

(and earn points from Jamie): "The heat, the humidity, the isolation, most newcomers can't stand it. They soon go back to wherever they've come from. It's different if you're born and bred here."

"Ah," Mr. Kilian said, clearly stimulated. "Precisely my point. People like you have adapted."

"Like the cattle have?" Jamie asked.

His father ignored him. "If the north can be made more attractive, whites will want to come here. White women will find conditions easier. Cooler homes. Proper dress and good food. Advances in tropical medicine. Abstinence from excessive drinking."

Jamie was stirred up now. "Who does all the work while we sit inside out of the sun, Dad?"

"Machinery," Mr. Kilian said. He was flushed, a little damp, a little sulky looking.

"And who works the machinery?" Jamie demanded.

"We may need some black workers," his father conceded.

"Won't they threaten your purity?"

"That's quite enough, Jamie."

We fell silent, but not for long. Mr. Kilian leaned over the table toward my father. "You're a pearler, Mike. I imagine you have thoughts on the Jap."

My father was guarded with him. "In what respect?"

"The Japs have been spying on us for years. Gaining the

measure of our emptiness and lack of preparation. The out-of-sight-out-of-mind way we approach things."

My father laughed. "You're saying my Japanese divers are all spies?"

"It makes sense. Japanese fleets and individuals have been allowed to come and go willy-nilly for forty or fifty years. They have eyes in their heads. But what your Jap *can't* measure is our willingness to fight."

Japan had invaded parts of China during the 1930s. There were people who feared that the Japanese had also set their sights on Australia. But I was bored with Kilian by now. Jamie was fuming, and his mother looked forlorn and embarrassed, as though she longed to be somewhere else, home in Perth, perhaps, where the sea winds rose in the late afternoon and swept her cares away.

•

Conversations such as this one were fairly typical with Mr. Kilian. I soon learned not to respond, for it only encouraged him, but it was harder for Jamie. I'd visit him, and if Kilian senior was there, I'd witness father and son locking horns in a sour, bitter, useless way, until voices were raised and Jamie came close to tears of rage, frustration, and shame. He would burst out of the house with me in tow, and power away on his short, strong legs toward the jetty, with me hurrying behind him, trying to keep up. I'd draw abreast of him and see his furious blinking eyes, his silent mouthing of the things he wished he'd said to his father.

I have to confess that seeing Jamie upset and vulnerable acted as an antidote to my own doubts and fears. The more human Jamie seemed, the less fearful I was about his intentions concerning Mitsy, and the less intimidated I was by his abilities.

I'd wanted to keep Jamie separate from Alice and Mitsy, fearing that he'd alter the composition of our lives, tip the balance one way or the other, but Alice and Mitsy couldn't see that anything personal was at stake. Alice felt sorry for Jamie. "That awful father," she said.

And so Alice, Mitsy, and I became Jamie Kilian's shelter from the storm. We let him into our lives, where he could be sharp and clever and restless, and not be quashed for it.

But I was on edge, waiting for disaster. In the darkness of the cinema in Sheba Lane, anything could have been happening. When the music rose and the breasts of the women swelled in passion, and they closed their eyes and kissed the hero, did Jamie sometimes sigh softly, sit back, and steal a hand along the back of Mitsy's seat, to touch and get close to her and breathe her in?

I had no way of knowing. Jamie would stretch his arms outside later, blinking in the sudden light, and say of whatever film we'd seen, "That was a load of rubbish," immediately setting off an argument with Mitsy and Alice, and I'd join in, but always with the suspicion that Jamie was trying to tease Mitsy, to make her laugh, make her notice him.

I hate that time in my life. I seemed to become someone unlike my true self. I became awkward, clumsy, tongue-tied. And when, at the end of the year, Alice and Mitsy left school to start as trainee nurses at the hospital, we four were apart more often, which offered opportunities for each of us to lead secret lives.

In my misery, I followed Jamie one day, certain that he was meeting Mitsy. But I was a poor shadow. I rounded a corner and he pounced on me. "Well, well, well, Hartley Penrose, fancy seeing you here."

I twisted out of his grasp. "What's going on between you and Mitsy?"

There was no humor in his smile. "You tell me."

"Are you seeing her?"

"That's my business."

"I've known her longer than you have."

It was a stupid argument, the kind you have when love is unrequited and you don't have all the facts. Anyway, Jamie laughed, not unkindly, and after a while I laughed too. He clamped an arm around my shoulders. "You're my mate, Hart."

Then he let me go and said, offhandedly, "There's your mother. She gets around."

I still don't know if he was being cruel or not, but several months had passed since his arrival in Broome, sufficient time for him to be aware of the town's secrets and heartaches. Someone had no doubt told him about my mother, her solitary walks, the suspicions that surrounded her. I broke away from him and went home.

That night Ida presented us with a telegram. "My father is dying," she said. "I have to go home."

The Phony War

Ida left us in March 1939, when the luggers were laid up and the storms chased one another in from the Indian Ocean. The Broome aerodrome was sodden, and the little aircraft taking my mother to Darwin steered a drunkard's path between the gluey mud patches, then almost clipped the trees at the end of the runway. We all let out a sigh when it finally climbed free of the earth, and I heard one brief, choked sob from my father.

"I won't be seeing her again."

That alarmed me. I'd taken it for granted that Ida would be coming back to us.

Alice took his arm. "Don't be silly, Dad."

"Oh, one day you kids will catch up with her, but that's it for me," he said.

We seemed to sleepwalk back to the Nash. My father said abruptly, "There's going to be a war."

•

My father meant war in Europe, for Hitler had just seized Prague, but there was also talk of war in the Pacific. Jamie Kilian's father had been shaking his finger in warning at anyone who would listen: "That pig iron we're selling to the Japs — it's going to come back to us as bullets and bombs. You mark my words."

"The old man, ranting and raving again," Jamie said.

But it wasn't as simple as that. We all noticed a change in Mitsy and her father as the talk of Japan and Japanese aims intensified. I'd always thought of Zeke as an ordinary, uncomplicated, hardworking man, bent by a lifetime of tough physical labor, and who'd not seen Japan for forty years. But in 1939 he was made secretary of the local Nihonjin-kai, a kind of Japanese social club and information center aimed at bridging the gap between Japan and Australia.

One day when Alice, Jamie, and I called in to collect Mitsy for a swim, we found Zeke counting a stack of one-pound and ten-shilling notes, silver florins, shillings, and sixpences, checking the amounts against names in a battered ledger. Mitsy was with him, typing a letter on an old type-writer with Japanese characters.

"What are you doing?" Alice asked.

Zeke waved at us without looking up. "Go away. Very busy here."

We turned to Mitsy. "Coming for a swim?"

"I'm helping Dad."

Zeke spoke to her rapidly in Japanese. She looked at us and explained, "Next year is the twenty-six-hundredth an-niversary of the Empire. We've taken up a collection to send home."

"Home?" Alice said, raising her eyebrows.

Mitsy scowled. "You know what I mean."

"Come for a swim."

"Later."

On other occasions we found Mitsy counting money for a defense contribution to Japan. She took it all very seri-ously. We teased her, but that only made her shut herself off from us, withdraw into the cultural traditions of a country she'd never seen. Once, when we went too far, she flashed, "I wish I were in Japan instead of this uncultivated dump."

"Why don't you just go then?" Alice retorted.

"I would if your father paid my father more."

That's what happens between friends. You rub too closely sometimes and the friction ignites the hidden grievances.

Mitsy apologized later. "Your dad's good to us," she said. "I didn't mean it."

Alice and I gestured carelessly. "Forget it. Come for a swim."

And we wandered down to the sweeping arc of Cable Beach and became ratty kids again.

•

Meanwhile there was a letter from Ida.

My darling Hartley and Alice, she wrote.

I miss you terribly and your smiling faces are always in my thoughts. I have sad news. Your grandfather died last week, and it's one of the disappointments of my life that you didn't have the opportunity to meet him. I know he would have been very fond of you. My mother needs me now, and so I will be staying on for the time being, but I must say that the daily war talk here is a drain on my spirits. I hope your father is keeping well. He was asking about your birth certificates. They are in the bottom drawer of the bureau in my sewing room.

We didn't know that he'd been writing to her.

•

A few months later, war broke out in Europe. For a time, until April of the following year, there was little fighting. It was called a phony war. Nevertheless, it would not have been easy for my mother to return, even if she'd wanted to.

Then, in quick succession, Germany invaded Denmark, Norway, Holland, Belgium, and France. By mid-1940, an air war was being fought in the skies over Britain. If I sound like a newsreel it's because that's the way we thought, conditioned by the dramatic voice-overs we heard in the prickly comfort of our seats in the tin cinema in Sheba Lane, as tanks rolled through villages and cannons recoiled and bomb craters smoked in the suburbs of London.

One night in January 1941, Jamie seemed to want to leap from his seat into the screen. He said, as we filed out later, "I'm going to join up."

Alice hooked her arm in his and pulled him against her hip. "My hero."

He shrugged her off in irritation. "England's in strife."

That's how people spoke. You didn't laugh at them. You read about the storm clouds over Europe and you shivered, you didn't scoff.

I saw Mitsy turn away. She looked troubled and confused. "Mitz?" I said.

"I'm going home. Good night," and she was gone.

I felt helpless. I could read her heart. If Japan joined the war, we'd be on opposite sides.

I've always needed time to ponder things. I needed to examine my feelings. I couldn't announce, as blithely as Jamie had done, that I intended to join up. Did I really want to go to war? If I joined up, would it be because I believed in a cause or because I didn't want Jamie to get all the praise and recognition? And what would Mitsy think? Would she see it as a hostile act?

I walked home, my head churning. To make it worse, Alice was excited by Jamie's announcement. She was practically skipping alongside me. "I could become an Army nurse," she said.

But another telegram was waiting for us. It brought bad news and drove all other thoughts out of our heads.

Storm Warning

My life has been a series of beginnings. A new life began in 1941, the year my mother was killed. That was also the year I turned nineteen, came close to drowning, and felt Mitsy Sennosuke's healing hands upon me for the first time, but, in early March, those things were still ahead of me. There was only my mother, and her manner of dying. I imagined the bomber and the whistling bomb, the flame-rip and the obliterating noise, and I told myself that surely she was thinking about us as the walls toppled and the roof beams came crashing down.

As if to underscore the pain, the Wet that year was suffocating, the winds and rain shutting us down for four long months. My father handled it badly. He was bored, he was broke, he was cranky, and mourning my mother. He needed to be at sea again.

On March 2, he weighed that need against the dangers of a late-season cyclone, and decided to take a chance. "Hart," he said, dragging me out of bed, "the Wet is over, I can feel it in my bones. Look at that sky! Look at the sea!"

We walked through the dawn light to Chinatown to raise Zeke. The Sennosukes were already awake and gave us green tea in their little kitchen. Sadako was sterilizing soy sauce bottles in a massive tub of boiling water. Mitsy was dressed for the day shift at the hospital, and darted in and out of the kitchen, complaining that she'd be late for work. Zeke was quietly smoking a cigarette, and wasn't convinced by my father's enthusiasm. He stepped out the back door, gazed at the cloud wisps on the horizon, came back inside, and said, "I don't know, boss," but didn't press the matter. Maybe he was eager for action too.

We woke the other divers and crew, rowed out to the *Ida Penrose*, waited until all five luggers were ready to go, and left Broome. We sailed south for three days, to Paterson Shoals, at the northern end of the Eighty Mile Beach, where we anchored in sixteen fathoms of water. The ocean bed shelves there at the rate of one fathom for every mile, and pearl oysters grow on the shelves in a band forty miles wide and five hundred miles long, fed by the tides of the Indian Ocean. The crew got ready. The divers descended.

We'd set out in fine conditions, but a northwesterly wind sprang up at mid-morning on that third day, increasing to gale force and finally hurricane strength. The shoreline was twenty miles away. I could just make out the five other luggers of our fleet, but through a lowering sky and a buffeting wind.

From time to time, my father checked the barometer. By noon he could no longer ignore what it was telling him. He tapped the glass one final time, went pale, and flew the storm-warning signal. "Mad," he said. "It was madness to linger."

We shortened sail and turned toward the shore. I was frightened by now. I was cold, soaked to the skin, numb, and senseless in the lashing wind. Twice I collided with Zeke on the foredeck. "Mr. Hart, you go inside now," he said, but I stayed on deck, crouched miserably in the shelter of the wheelhouse. In the darkness and the heaving sea, we had lost all sight of the other luggers.

At three o'clock, when we were still about six miles out, the full force of the cyclone hit us. All we could do was let a couple of anchors go, take off the top hamper, fasten the hatches, and ride it out. The crew went below. Zeke joined my father and me in the cabin. I tapped the barometer —

27.72 degrees. My father raised his hands to his face in dismay. He'd never seen it so low. "I've put you all in danger," he said. "Sorry, Zeke, sorry, son."

I grew alarmed. Were we going to die?

Then the wind dropped. The *Ida Penrose* continued to pitch and yaw, as if she might break open, but the howling was gone from our ears. We were in the windless eye of the storm, suffering a strange, silent, ceaseless battering, and I remember that I felt acutely attuned to disaster, waiting for the wind to revisit us. "Rum," said my father, breaking out a bottle. We had three tots each during that long wait. It burned inside me.

Suddenly my father jumped to his feet. "What was I thinking? You're both blue with cold," he said, and he forced us to change into dry clothes. If I turn my eyes inward, I can see Zeke in faded pajamas, my father in a heavy overcoat, and me in overalls. I wonder what Zeke thought about those pajamas. Pajamas seem too benign for a man who had led a hazardous life and died a violent death.

We sat and waited. Now and then we jabbered excitedly, remembering something funny or risky from the past, but mostly we were waiting. Once my father asked, his face a little embarrassed, "Zeke, you don't think Japan will invade, do you?"

"What for him do that?" Zeke said.

At five o'clock the winds hit again, southeasterly this time, striking with enough force to tip the *Ida Penrose* on to her side. I heard the ballast shift, and found myself kneeling on the starboard wall of the cabin, my father crouched next to me. Zeke was somewhere behind us. I had no thoughts in my head beyond our tipped-over world, but Zeke and my father acted immediately. They opened the scuttle and pushed me through it.

But at that point, before I fell free of the scuttle and out onto the deck, the *Ida Penrose* shuddered as if to rid herself of me. I felt a rip of pain in my leg, then I was snatched by a breasting roller. It took me fathoms beneath the surface, then up again, other rollers repeating the action until I thought I'd die.

Zeke found me. I suddenly felt the powerful wrap of his left arm around my chest, and for the next twelve hours we rode the sea together, Zeke scooping with his right arm, his legs scissoring, keeping my head out of the water. It was not until daybreak, in the easing of the wind and the waves, that our feet touched bottom.

We came ashore at Cape Latouche Treville. I don't recall much after that. All I remember is waking and sitting up and patting the sand next to me, searching for Zeke but feeling only sand, and hearing only the scrape of the sea, and realizing, from the sun's rays on the surface of my eyelids, that it was midday, not midnight, and I was blind. I tried to shout Zeke's name. My voice sounded puny, as if this were a nightmare and no words would come.

It was surf blindness. It lasted for two days. I heard and felt but could not see the station blacks who massaged life into my bones. Their camp had vanished in the wind and they'd been wandering along the shoreline, searching for jetsam, when they found me. I heard and felt but could not see the doctor and the nurses who cared for me in Broome. I had no need of my eyes to know that Alice and Mitsy were tending to me, or to know that my left leg had been scraped open from thigh to ankle.

Chambers of the Deep

Nurses in a rough-and-ready town like Broome have seen everything. They are disinclined to let you feel sorry for yourself. I can remember the coarse-grained towel around my neck, the sensation of over-soaked cotton wool attacking my caked and swollen eyelids, the runnels of hot salty water along my jawline and down inside my collar, the busy fingers exploring my torn leg, the constant jollying along. My complaints were swatted away like so many flies. It was as if I had a duty to grow up quickly in a country where the frontier snatches your loved ones away from you. But if the treatment was crude, it was effective, and when I was finally able to see again I made a feeble joke: "You're a sight for sore eyes!"

It was the matron, and she rocked back on her heels in amusement. "Am I indeed? Then here's another sight for them."

She stepped aside to reveal my father — and Alice, in her nurse's uniform. They were as alike as twins, tall and flesh-less, and I saw them float toward me in a watery light, and lean close to my head. I closed my eyes; they planted their lips on my cheeks.

Then the matron's voice came to me in snatches, as though I still had salt water in my ears: ". . . been badly scratched, Mr. Penrose . . . swollen and weepy . . . walk again . . . plenty of exercise."

A short time later she shoecreaked away and I opened my eyes and found Alice. "I want Ida," I said.

To this day, I don't know why I said it. I'm sure that I hadn't been thinking of our mother at that moment. It may be that I wanted to cause consternation, or hurt the feelings of my father, for driving her away to a place where she would be killed by a bomb, and for taking me to sea when it was not safe to do so, and it may be that I wanted my mother's arms around me again.

Alice took charge. She ceased being my young sister and became nurse-like: "Now, now, Hartley. We want you to hurry up and get better for us."

And my father said, "You're not to worry about anything, son. You're in good hands here."

My emotions were topsy-turvy. How could I tell these two efficient, bossy people that I wanted only to be held tightly for a while?

I changed the subject. I didn't mention Ida again. Instead, I simply said Zeke's name. He was there in my head whenever I slept and whenever I awoke. His strong arm, his ceaseless fortifying voice in my ear, the sensation of my head tucked under his chin.

Alice glanced uneasily at my father. "They're still looking for him."

"Looking for him?"

My father pushed both hands back through his thick hair. He was agitated. "The *Argyle* picked me up. They'd seen Zeke in the water with Lefinas, but then lost sight of them. We didn't know that you were safe."

I closed my eyes. "Does Mitsy know?"

"Yes."

"Simeon? Bin?"

"We haven't found them."

I began to gasp, as though there were not enough air left in the world. "The other luggers?"

My father was relieved to be giving me good news after

so much bad. "They all made it back safely, but there were losses in some of the other fleets."

We were silent. I could hear the ceiling fan and the coughs and murmurs of other patients, and the distant squabbling of birds in the palm trees. My eyes snapped open. "Zeke warned us. He said he didn't like the look of the sky, remember?"

My father seemed to roll his body in pain. Alice leaned over the narrow iron bed until her face was close to mine, and she began to stroke my temples. "Hush. We don't know that Zeke's dead. He could have washed up somewhere and be heading home even as we speak."

"No he's not."

After a while my father spoke again. His voice was strained. "Hart, I have to see how Sadako is. I'll be in again this afternoon, all right?" And he hurried out.

Alice hurried after him. For a long time then I lay there, looking out at the grounds of the hospital. The air was stifling. I dozed.

•

When I awoke, Mitsy was sitting on a fold-up wooden chair next to the bed.

"You look hot, Hart."

I sat upright. The movement wrenched my leg and the

pain was so intense that sweat popped on my scalp and flowed down my face. "Mitz."

"You look hot," she said again.

"I'm so sorry about Zeke."

She turned away. After a while she murmured, "It's not knowing that's the hard part. If we had a body, we could have a burial."

"How's your mum taking it?"

"I wish I spoke better Japanese," Mitsy said. Tears formed in her eyes. "I can't tell her exactly what *I'm* feeling and she can't tell me exactly what *she's* feeling. We don't seem to connect very well."

"My father should never have taken the fleet out."

Her hand snapped over my mouth. "Don't. No one's blaming your father."

I struggled, determined to articulate the guilt I was feeling, but Mitsy clamped her hand tighter over my mouth, looked fiercely down at me, and said warningly, "Hart, don't, I mean it."

At last she took her hand away.

She stood and drew a curtain around the bed. "Time for your bath."

I was alarmed. I didn't want Alice or Mitsy to bathe me. I didn't see how they could be professionally neutral about it. I'd grown up with them, after all. They couldn't be neutral about my bare skin, my nakedness. And I'd wanted to be Mitsy's lover for so long that I feared my body would betray me, and that she'd turn away, scornful or amused or indifferent or in clear disgust.

"Can't someone else do it?"

She stripped back the sheet. I was wearing hospital-issue short pajamas, and her fingers began to flick down the buttons of the pajama top. "We're short-staffed and overworked this week. There are a dozen men in here from other lugger fleets, all with injuries after that storm."

Soon I was naked and Mitsy had rolled me onto a towel and begun to sponge me with a damp cloth. It was both better and worse than I thought it would be. I was concentrating so hard on not becoming aroused that I didn't at first realize that Mitsy was treating me as if I were just another patient. She chatted, her motions gentle, bathing me with long, cooling strokes of the washcloth around the hot, tight dressings on my torn leg. Slowly I relaxed.

But then she began to hum, then to grin, and finally she gave me a featherlight flick with her fingers and said, fighting down the giggles, "At least your old boy wasn't torn off."

In answer, my "old boy" sprang up. Mitsy laughed then, a bawdy but not unkind laugh. I wish I'd had the wits to laugh along with her, but I groaned and tried to cover myself and turn away from her. I was hot-faced and ashamed. Finally, it all seemed wrong. We didn't know if Zeke were alive or dead, wandering hurt on a lonely shore or caught beneath the deep.

Suddenly I heard a sob. The humor faded from Mitsy's face, as if she'd read my thoughts. She stopped sponging me. Her forehead dropped onto my knee. I couldn't see her face. She was inconsolable and it was more than I could bear. I stretched down until I could cup her bare neck with my hand, and I whispered her name.

Mitsy lifted her head. "Hart, I feel lost."

Coastwatch

I remained in the ward for a further three weeks. Every day I was stung, by the hard, brassy, arms-swinging air of the nurses, into exercising my leg. I'm sure that they saved it — saved me — from atrophying. I was given no time to feel sorry for myself, or be alone. My father visited every day. He was selling his remaining luggers, he said.

"My heart's not in it anymore, son. And I want to give something to Sadako and the other widows."

Kids from school visited. The first time Jamie came by, he seemed a little awkward, a little tentative. "I've been accepted by the Air Force. I train in Canada, then get posted somewhere."

I suppose that's what friends do, tell one another their good fortune, but this was the kind of good fortune I could never aspire to now, not with my injured leg. Jamie wasn't being unkind, he wasn't rubbing it in, but if we were never quite equal, we were now even further apart. To make it worse, he'd end every visit with the words, "Mitsy on duty today?"

And there was Alice, kind and smiling, popping her head into the ward several times a day to see how I was getting along.

But it was Mitsy I lived for. When she bathed me, a kind of sad longing seemed to flow from her into me. It was as if she needed to heal, to negate death. She would smile at me, a distant, abstracted smile. She was the opposite of the bossy nurses.

As the days mounted, however, and no news came of her father, she grew more and more withdrawn. She began to accept that Zeke would never be found alive. Was she imagining how he'd be found in death? Wedged in a reef somewhere, his limbs snapped like twigs and his features sodden and bloated, the skin lifting away? Or blackening on a forgotten stretch of sand, food for the crabs and the seabirds? She was clearly grieving, but the configuration of it was private, and I longed for her to talk to me.

An opportunity came one morning after she'd been away

for three days. I was a little frantic as a result. The shameful side of me said that she had no right to abandon me. The generous side said that of course she needed time alone to grieve, and to care for Sadako.

When she walked in I burst out, "I've missed you."

Mitsy looked past me and fussed with the sheet at the foot of my bed. "My mother needed me."

I was about to say, "I needed you too," the kind of response you make when you're upset and selfish and not thinking straight, but I stopped myself in time.

"How is she?"

"She's not coping very well."

I sat up straight in the bed. "My father's selling his fleet, everything but his dinghy. He'll be able to give her some money soon."

Mitsy frowned crossly, as if to say, "For God's sake," and I saw that I'd offended her with my mention of money, as though money could stave off grief. I said hurriedly, "I walked twice up and down the corridor today."

"Good."

Mitsy was not looking at me. Her mind was far away. Suddenly she said, "No one understands. We need the body."

I reached out and she let me close my hand over hers. It felt hot and alive but as tight as a rock. Her whole body was agitated. I knew, from my father's years of pearling, how important it was to the Japanese divers to bring a corpse back for burial. I'd heard of whole fleets stopping work and sailing home to Broome to bury a dead Japanese diver, even if they were seven days' sailing time away. Burial on land, in the home port, showed a proper respect for the dead. You did not bury a man like Zeke at sea on the pearling grounds, but that's what had happened, in effect. To Sadako — and even to Mitsy, modern Mitsy — Zeke was lost.

"Is there some kind of prayer?" I asked. "Some kind of ceremony to save him?"

"Oh, Hart."

Mitsy knuckled both of her eyes and stood up. I sensed that I'd said something right this time, that I'd struck the right note, to acknowledge the *Japanese* side of Mitsy's nature.

Then she said, "Hart, my mother needs me."

"Of course."

"I don't think you understand. I'm quitting work to be with her."

•

Eventually my father fetched me home in the black Nash, and I fell into a sad, subdued, almost pleasant kind of dreaminess. I thought that the world was full of busybodies and I retreated in the face of all that good cheer. I had no need of speech or action but curled up with books and day-dreams in corners of the house where the filtered light barely caught the dust motes and no sounds penetrated.

At first I reread all the books that my mother had so hated: those memoirs by old bushmen, biographies of camelback clergymen, descriptions of motorcar journeys across trackless wastes the size of Europe, crackpot schemes to flood the inland, naturalists' rambles, popular anthropology, and travelers' tales by visiting journalists who'd sped through, looked, and written a book.

They were pretty predictable books. Size was always remarked upon: the Canning Stock Route was almost nine hundred miles long; the rise and fall of the tides in King Sound had been measured at forty feet; just three hundred people lived on the thirty-nine cattle stations of the West Kimberley, an area the size of Victoria; Vesteys, the English pastoral company, signed up leases for an area larger than Tasmania before the Great War; Jubilee Downs, 190 miles inland from Derby, carried fifteen thousand head of cattle on one million acres.

There were unremitting deserts and tropical coasts, pearls and government wells, the half-mile Broome jetty and the Derby boab tree, crazed lonely prospectors and steadfast troopers of the Northwest Mounted Police, the part-Aboriginal question and the dying out of the old Dark People, the empty, misunderstood north and the ignorant south.

It was like being stuck in a room with Jamie Kilian's father, being beaten about the head with his coast-watching preoccupations. According to those books, no one knew the sacrifices we made, as we hung on up there, in Unknown Australia, in the Never Never, in the Great Unfenced, before the age of hurry-up. We were the true Australians, in a country going begging, ruled by governments, cities, and absentee landlords who knew nothing and cared less about resource development, soil erosion, and the teeming threat of Asia, which sat right on our back doorstep, waiting, waiting. . . .

One day I simply closed the book I was reading and tossed it across the room. It flapped like an injured bird and fell torn into a corner. I reached for Ida's *Oliver Twist*. I wanted to be taken out of myself.

A curious thing happened: the terrains of England began to impinge on my consciousness, altering, then effacing, the world outside the library window. I was pleased, and a little alarmed. After a while, the alarm receded; I was wrapped in a pleasurable dreaminess. I was in a better place. If true life existed elsewhere, then I had almost found it. I tried not to think of Mitsy.

Nerve Ghosts

It was Alice who saw me through. She took two weeks off work to be with me. My father was no help. He went to Darwin to negotiate with a Japanese pearling company at one stage, but mostly sat staring at the water from the doorway of the chandlery store.

For the first few days, Alice was unobtrusive, deliberately marking time, matching her moods and her daily rhythms to mine as a way of helping me to recover. Then, by degrees, she began to work on me. She made me talk, and she massaged my legs, using techniques that Sadako had shown her, and she made me walk and stretch a little more each day. "Exercise," she said. "Exercise, exercise, exercise."

I complied. Gradually I spent less time reading or loung-
ing and more time hobbling about Broome on my injured
leg with the aid of a stick. The bad leg is shorter than the
other by an inch, which has skewed my lower back, so that
I have lived in pain ever since that time, and it's thinner and
badly scarred, but I tried to tell myself — and I still tell
myself, even now, when my leg twitches and nerve ghosts
jump in it, and door frames and garden gates remind me
of my tight, scraping escape through the scuttle on the *Ida
Penrose* — that at least I could walk, at least I was still alive.

I was grateful for Alice's closeness and attention. In the
years since our rough-and-tumble childhood, I had come to
take her for granted. She'd simply been my sister, simply
younger than me, and simply Mitsy Sennosuke's best friend.
Now I took notice of her.

She was beautiful and given to showy disasters or glori-
ous triumphs, but plain at heart. She was easy to read:
desire, compassion, envy, anger, hurt, and love were clearly
there, on her face or in her manner. And in a town so small,
Alice was noticed and talked about. Most people smiled
when they mentioned her. Most people loved her. If anyone
didn't it was because they found her too quick, too nimble,
too fierce, too clever, too contestable, or simply too desir-
able. There are young women like Alice in every small town,
itching to burn across the sky and never come back, but Alice

was in ours, and suddenly I was closer to her than I had been since we were little.

We talked about our mother, and why she hadn't come back. We talked about our father. We agreed that he was doubly suffering — first Ida, lying dead in bomb rubble, then the loss of Zeke and the other men. He was blaming himself and there was nothing we could do to stop him.

And we talked about Alice herself. "I'm leaving Broome," she said one day.

I was alarmed. "What do you mean?"

"I want to do something useful. The Army needs nurses."

I felt panicky. "Will Mitsy go with you?"

Alice was silent for some time. She hung her head so that her voice was muffled. "Mitsy is part of the reason why I'm leaving. She's cut me out of her life."

I laughed without much humor. "Join the club."

Alice lifted her head. "It's difficult. If I visit, Sadako doesn't say anything, just sits and stares. She's stopped working for Dad, and makes soy sauce only when she feels like it. As for Mitsy, she's very distant with me, as if I'm to blame. She even said once that I was lucky. Huh! I don't feel lucky."

"Alice," I burst out, "I'm in love with her."

"God, Hart, that's been obvious for years."

I fell silent. I was thinking stupid things. I thought that Alice might go around and talk sense into her, and that everyone would recognize and celebrate the aptness of a love between myself and Mitsy. You think things like that when you're in love. You don't see the world as it really is.

•

Our next news of Mitsy and Sadako came from our father. He returned from a trip to Port Hedland to say that he'd found a buyer for his luggers. He snorted: "I got peanuts. The world wants guns these days, not pearls."

From the proceeds of the sale he gave one thousand pounds each to Sadako and the widows of the other men who'd drowned on the *Ida Penrose*. Meeting Sadako and Mitsy again in such circumstances, he said, was terribly awkward and uncomfortable.

"Sadako didn't seem to comprehend what the money was for. Mitsy explained it to her, but that didn't make it any better." He lifted a pearlshell ashtray from the table as though it might offer wisdom. "I don't know, the money seemed to offend Mitsy. She was quite rude. She said that almost a thousand Broome divers have died over the years, as if it were my fault." He scratched his head, bewildered. "How would she come upon a statistic like that?"

•

Jamie left in April. I mentally mapped his journey: by air in a MacRobertson-Miller Lockheed to Darwin, then by Qantas flying-boat to Java, and from there in stages to England and finally Canada, a young man among the many who were flocking to the defense of the Empire in 1941.

My feelings were complicated. I envied him, I was jealous, I pitied myself. Perhaps that's why I decided not to go out to the aerodrome with Alice to say good-bye. I didn't want to witness the bounce in his step.

He left at dawn. Alice came back many hours later, flushed and elated. "You won't believe this," she said, "but I'm in love."

Burn Across the Sky

As Alice described it, she'd kissed Jamie good-bye, then stood apart from his parents in the sparse shade of an old Gypsy Moth, away from the pulsing heat of the iron shed at the aerodrome, waving from time to time as the aircraft warmed its engines, her other hand protecting her eyes from the sun. Several minutes passed, and then she became aware that the two men standing nearby in the dawn light were negotiating on the sale of the Gypsy Moth. One of them was Carl Venning, and he was exhilarated, rising onto his toes as he counted ten-pound banknotes into the palm of the other man. It was almost as if gravity couldn't contain him.

"Two hundred," he said.

Alice told me that he'd been watching her from the corner of his eye. He tilted his chin to indicate the Moth. "A spin, Alice?"

She was no longer the scrappy kid who used to hang over the front gate whenever Venning came by to drop Derby Boxer at our house. She was eighteen now. Venning was twenty-eight. She found herself saying yes, infected by his excitement. His eyes shone and the sun lit his hair. A man like that might never die, and that was the antidote she needed just then, an antidote to Mitsy and grieving.

The Moth carried the markings of the Vacuum Oil Company and signs of having worked hard in hard terrain. It was an open, two-seater biplane, and handled skittishly on the takeoff. The wind tore at Alice's hair; the wires hummed; the horizon tilted crazily; and Carl Venning's helmet, goggles, and leather jacket bore traces of tobacco, oil, and perspiration, suggesting our father to her.

At dusk, Carl returned her to the ground, before heading south along the coast to Hartog Downs. Alice watched the diminishing speck and wondered if he would beat the darkness home. Within minutes, the sky had swollen with stars, an eyeblink flooding of darkness that is a phenomenon of this part of the world.

Carl Venning was back the next morning, flushed and

damp, his boots muddy, laughing that he'd walked all the way in from the aerodrome and not seen a soul. My father was down at the chandlery, and so Carl seemed to fill our house, prowling about the sitting room, pausing to gaze through the broad windows at Roebuck Bay, and peering at the photographs on the walls.

"Your mother?"

"Yes."

"Ah. And who's the Jap?"

I was a little cool with him. "Zeke Sennosuke."

Carl pointed at me and clicked his tongue. "Kept you alive in the water?"

I touched the bandages on my leg self-consciously. "Yes."

He turned away. "Come for a spin, Alice."

I didn't like him — he was too tall, rangy, and overconfident, a man careless of the feelings of others — but I tried to see what Alice saw in him. He seemed vacuous to me. Perhaps Alice had first seen him in a trick of the light, and, like all first impressions, it had been indelible and unalterable: his shapely head, his wide grin, his air of seeking freedom above the clouds, and the white horse-kick scar across his left eyebrow, so that he looked a little dangerous. He was vivid and easy to read, with a sun-glow on his arms and his face, and I was sure that there was nothing to him. I tried not to think of his two good legs.

But Alice liked him, and he was good for her. When eventually they became lovers, I could see it in the language of their bodies. Carl, I knew, was Alice's first lover. He lifted up her spirits. And my father liked him, responding to his vigor and optimism. So I tried to examine exactly why it was that I disliked Carl Venning.

Because he walked with a bounce. Because he'd always been snide about Derby whenever he dropped him at our front gate. Because he acted as though nothing had ever gone wrong for him, or ever would. He even crashed the Gypsy Moth on takeoff at dusk one afternoon, clipping the trees at the end of the aerodrome, and walked away from the wreckage without a scratch. He claimed he'd been avoiding a kangaroo, but he'd spent the day with Alice, in her bedroom while our father was at the chandlery store, and so I thought sourly that he was drunk on love and lovemaking, and had lost his judgment. He sold the Gypsy Moth for scrap and immediately bought a Puss Moth, a cabin monoplane with room for three. He was a wealthy man.

Then one morning, Alice came to my room, full of mystery, and said, "Pack an overnight bag. We're going on a trip."

Three hours later, I was airborne. First, Alice and Carl flew me over the Lacepede Islands, where, in the cyclone that killed Zeke, other luggers had foundered and other men had drowned. From the islands we headed inland along King Sound and the Fitzroy River, then landed to refuel at Halls Creek. Our final stop for the day was Wyndham. Alice had reserved rooms for us at the Bonaparte Hotel.

After that trip, I often flew with Carl and Alice. I was the world's witness to their giddy love, and to the local conditions at the town and station airstrips of the northwest. Soon we were well-known, and well-regarded, in an amused, indulgent way. We were a kind of traveling show. For three months in 1941, the Broome to Darwin record was ours. We searched for fliers lost in the desert country. We delivered the Royal Mail. We circumnavigated the continent twice. To mark Carl's twenty-ninth birthday, we flew the Puss Moth to Tjilatjap, on the island of Java, and holidayed at a hill station for ten days, indistinguishable from the colonial officials of Batavia in our white cotton.

We even flew a Sydney newspaper hack around for a couple of weeks. She was writing a travel book and wanted to see Beagle Bay Mission Station, the big pastoral properties along the Fitzroy River and the Buccaneer Archipelago. I bought a copy of her book for my father. It didn't seem to be about us — or only about us through tinted glass — and was full of local subversions. We heard later that she'd spent a few days with Eddie Horsetalk and Spinaway Sullivan in the front bar of the Roebuck Arms Hotel, and had solemnly reproduced every lie, tall story, and exaggeration they'd told her.

I felt no closer to Carl Venning. I tolerated him, for Alice's sake. He was a twinkling whistler, a grinning charmer, a man bursting with energy, and clearly in love with her. It was the flying I lived for. It elevated me from moodiness and inaction, and helped me to forget Mitsy.

I loved the stomach-lurch of our takeoffs from unfamiliar airstrips, the new day delivering us to a new horizon, the sense of danger. There were times when we put down on deserted beaches with engine trouble, but all I can remember of them is Carl winding up his portable gramophone in the shade of the wings and reaching into the engine bay with an oily rag, Alice sitting with her back to the landing wheel, half smiling and drowsy with love, and me keeping the logbook of the little plane up-to-date or watching the seabirds bank against the blue sky.

•

My first view of Hartog Downs, Carl Venning's home on the Broome to Port Hedland road, was from the air. Carl flew low over small, eroded outcrops of red stone and clumps of scrubby trees and patches of dry grass, and finally swooped over a rise to give a sudden view of the homestead. It was like finding a village in the wilderness: main house, visitors' quarters, workers' quarters, storeroom, meat house, work-shop, generator shed, garage, stockyards, shearing shed, garden, windmill, iron Furphy tanks, troughs, and airstrip.

When the Puss Moth landed, Derby Boxer came out to greet us. I'd not seen him for more than a year, and was reminded of a hank of toughened rope. The sun had dried him, hard work had kept him underweight and stiff in the joints, and he wore a work shirt, trousers, boots, and felt hat the color of dust. He looked dented and scarred by his life of cattle branding and horseback mustering.

He tipped back his hat. I saw a face creased with tired smile lines. When I held my hand out he didn't shake it but took my kitbag and carried it toward the veranda steps. "Bern sends her love, Derby," I called.

He paused but didn't turn around. "Thanks, boss."

I couldn't read him. In Broome he'd always been relaxed with us. I looked at the main house and outbuildings. There was a wireless mast for the pedal transceiver radio. Hens pecked about under poinciana trees. A goat snickered in a holding pen next to the slaughtering shed. I was tired, and in pain.

Then I felt Carl's arm around my shoulders. "Don't go getting too friendly with Derby. He's been a disappointment to me."

We mounted the steps and entered the house, where

Tilly, Carl's house girl, had tea waiting. I have a memory of dim, cool rooms, handmade hardwood and crocodile-hide chairs, a wine cellar, mounted buffalo horns in the dining room, a Martini-Henry elephant rifle on the wall of Carl's study, and a library furnished with leather armchairs, a windup gramophone, a baby grand piano, and walls of crack-spined books. It wasn't an untidy house, but it did wear a faint patina of dust and neglect, as though Carl would stand in doorways from time to time and stare helplessly in on unused rooms and long for a wife.

The Desired Earth

I saw things on my travels with Alice and Carl that year that I didn't see on Hartog Downs. For example, Carl didn't force his recalcitrant black stockmen to dress in women's clothing and do women's work. He wasn't interested in hiring Europeans who were prized for being tough on the blacks. There was no servant woman pulling a cord to fan him at dinner or in his club chair in the evenings. If the blacks got "cheeky" he might dock their wages but never chain them down on a corrugated iron roof or stir the loose flour, tea, and sugar together in one billy can on ration day. He didn't play the role of pimp and send black maids to the visitors' quarters, something that some managers did for company men visiting from London. I never saw him horse-whip anyone or heard him raise his voice.

Carl was also the leaseholder of Hartog Downs, and worked the property himself. Most of the Kimberley stations were leased to English companies with interests in Argentina, North America, and northern Australia, or to syndicates in Adelaide and Melbourne. Their managers belonged to a virtuous, powerful, and mostly unaccountable elite. They dressed for dinner, sold luxuries at inflated prices in the station store, paid low wages to the stockmen and domestic servants, asked the troopers to bring back runaway workers, overstocked a vast tract of land with the wrong breed of cattle, and did nothing that might lower white prestige in the north.

Even so, Hartog Downs was a kind of feudal enclave, and Carl ruled it with a firm hand. In the mustering season it supported more than thirty people. Five were European: Carl himself, a married couple who managed the books and the storeroom, an engineer, and a cook who doubled as the butcher. The remainder were Aboriginal: stockmen, headed by Derby Boxer, domestic servants, and station blacks. Some, like Derby and Tilly, lived in permanent quarters. The station blacks followed the mustering camps and otherwise lived in bark shelters on a dustflat some distance from the homestead for eight months of the year, and on ceremonial sites and hunting grounds during the Wet.

My uneasiness about Carl Venning was strengthened one weekend when his neighbors, a married couple named Lester and Olive Webb, came to dinner at Hartog Downs. Because they lived two hours north, they would not drive back afterward but spend the night in the visitors' quarters.

Carl was anxious for us to meet them, but I disliked Lester Webb on first sight. He looked like a back alley skulker, the way he seemed to hunch his thin shoulders and swing his narrowed eyes left and right. He spoke in a hurried mutter, always biting off unnecessary words: "Bogged to the axles . . . good thrashing . . . cheeky bugger."

He called his wife "mate," "matey," or "cobber." Olive looked as if she'd been worn to the bone by isolation and silence, and resembled Lester in a harried, careworn way, but without his air of cunning, or his snatched, corner-of-the-mouth speech.

She was unhappy. I've met many station women like Olive Webb, women whose loneliness, frustration, and sense of injustice can never find a direct voice. They are rarely allowed to complain or criticize. They are married to men whose expectations are clear: never interfere in the work of the menfolk but make the house a haven from worry; provide good food and clean surroundings; treat the servants and the yard boys fairly but firmly; and be wife, mother, sister, nurse, and mate.

As the evening progressed, Olive grew sharp and didactic. She began to lecture Alice, as if to prepare her for married life in the station country: "Leniency breeds contempt, Alice. Your average blacks respect a firm hand. They're naturally lazy. Hard work is a fool's game to them. You must never let them get cheeky. If they do, step in quick-smart and squash it."

Tilly was collecting our plates. I looked at her in embarrassment, hoping that she hadn't been offended, but she was expressionless. She might have been offended, she might have been in silent agreement because a white woman was saying it, or she might not have been listening. It was only later that I saw her mimicking Olive's skinny, scurrying walk and purse-mouthed disapproval. If subversion was her only defense against the Webbs of her world, it was effective.

"Your blackfellow can't make ethical or moral distinctions," Olive went on. "He can't understand things like mercy or kindness. In his native state he's quite resourceful, but does he ever carry that through to something bigger or better? No. It's baffling."

I looked at Alice. She was staring at something far away, as if at her future. On the other side of the table, Carl Venning beamed at her benignly.

•

In the weeks that followed the dinner with the Webbs, Alice grew edgy and distracted. One day in July, five minutes after we'd landed at Hartog Downs for a weekend's visit, she came to my room. I'd unpacked my kitbag, and was sitting rubbing my leg when she entered without knocking, looking troubled:

"He wants a wife."

"That's obvious, Al."

"Everyone's taking it for granted that we'll get married."

"Don't you want to?"

"Yes. No. I don't know. Can you imagine having to be friendly to the Webbs?"

"Alice, no one's forcing you to marry him."

She folded her arms. "I meant it when I said I want to be an Army nurse."

"I know you did. Why not ask Carl to wait for you?"

Alice laughed abruptly. "He hasn't even popped the question yet."

•

The next morning, Alice asked me to walk with her to the top of the only hill near the homestead. We stood for a while, staring out at the Indian Ocean to the west, the baking basalt plains to the east, and after some time noticed a sluggish dust cloud on the approach road to Hartog Downs. It was caused by a black sedan, a small, dark shape at that distance, which braked at the homestead ramp before turning in. We watched it as it crept around the parched lawn and parked next to the steps of the main house. I recognized Lester Webb's long, snouty Packard, and said, "Not those two again."

Alice groaned.

A uniformed Army officer emerged from the passenger side of the car. "I wonder what's going on?" Alice said. "Maybe the Japs have landed and no one's told us."

"I don't think that's very funny," I said.

"Aren't you the touchy one," she said. "Is it Mitsy? Mitsy's turned her back on us."

"It's not easy for her."

"So what? She's lost her father, we've lost our mother."

"You know it's more than that."

Alice stormed ahead, reaching the bottom of the hill before me. Here she waited, watching my queer, dipping shuffle as though she hated it. "Carl asked me to marry him this morning."

I stopped, panting, forearming the sweat away from my eyes. "Is that why you're so cranky? Don't marry him."

"Why not?"

"I don't like him."

She snorted. "Hypocrite. You don't like him, yet you're happy to be his guest."

"Did you say yes?"

In answer, she turned away and continued along the track toward the airstrip, striding out, swiping at the pandanus palms and turkey bush with her sun hat.

She was right. I was a hypocrite. I waited until Alice was out of sight. I didn't want her to turn around and see me hobbling after her.

I found Alice and Carl and our visitors drinking tea on the veranda, screened from the glare by the old madeira vine. Lester Webb gazed past me, then down at the veranda boards, and muttered my name to the Army officer, who was a scrubbed pink, balding man named Morrissey.

"The major is here to help us, Hart," Alice said. Her gaze and her voice were too level. She was warning me about something, or she was being ironic.

I said, "I see," and turned to Morrissey for an explanation.

"We're forming a Volunteer Defense Corps," he said. "Armed guerrilla bands, here in the pastoral country, could be very useful."

"How?" Alice demanded.

Morrissey ignored her. "One of our main fears is what

the Abo might do. We can't evacuate him. The Minister won't let us round him up. If the Japs land, you know what'll happen."

"Do we?" I said.

"Your Abo is unreliable," Morrissey said. "He'll collaborate. He'll guide the Japs through the bush."

"Rubbish," Alice said.

Morrissey began to get red in the face. "We've had reports of smoke signals on remote parts of the coast. You've got old links between Japanese pearlers and the coastal tribes. If your Jap painted his face with burnt cork, who would be the wiser?"

Alice snorted. "You're mad. Clear off. Go on, clear off."

But Morrissey jerked his chair close to Carl Venning's and leaned forward, his forearms on his knees: "Look, the Abos are going to be a liability if the Japs land. Some will choose to collaborate. The renegade, the malingerer, the fellow you sacked last month. He'll guide the Japs through the bush in exchange for grog and tobacco." He sat back. "Even if we *can* trust the blacks, how are we going to look after them?"

Carl pursed his lips. He was taking Morrissey's point seriously. "But how capable are the Japs? What I heard, they're all shortsighted. Guns don't work. Bamboo planes."

"What would you know?" I said.

"Readiness is the key," Morrissey said, as if I hadn't spoken. "And they invaded China, don't forget."

"Point."

"Jap luggers have been seen off Broome. Do you think they're sunning themselves? No. They're watching us."

Alice folded her arms. "I can't believe I'm hearing two grown men talking like this."

Morrissey continued to ignore her. "It's the black with a chip on his shoulder I'm worried about. He could easily infect a lot of others. He's got to be nipped in the bud."

"You have no idea," Alice said.

Finally Morrissey swung around on her. "A man could be excused for thinking you don't have our defense needs at heart."

"Hear, hear," Lester Webb muttered.

"Carl, tell these men they're not welcome here."

But Carl Venning ignored her. "Let's say we do form a local defense unit, what would our role be?"

It was Lester Webb who answered him, as if he knew that Morrissey would be unlikely to say more in front of Alice. He leaned forward, in a gesture dark and collaborative. "You won't find this written down anywhere, but if the Abos cause trouble we can shoot them, no questions asked."

Alice recoiled. "You stupid, ugly little man. I'm not going to listen to any more of this."

When she was gone, Carl Venning said, "Leave her, I'll talk to her. She'll see sense in the end."

"A wife like that could be a liability, Carl," Lester Webb said.

"I'll make sure she isn't."

I limped away.

"What about you, son?" Morrissey called. "A gammy leg needn't be an impediment. You could have an office role, do wireless work, gather intelligence . . ."

I didn't reply. I felt choked. Eventually I heard the Packard drive away, probably headed for the next property. Alice was in the library, just standing there, blinking her eyes. I told her what had been said after she stormed off, and she led me back to the veranda, where, with icy control, she asked Carl to fly us back to Broome.

He didn't argue. He saw something final in my sister that day, and some of the light went out of his eyes, and he didn't contact her again.

Hard Liberty

Alice shook off what she now called the jaunty and trifling side of herself, interested only in one man's grin and the next dawn takeoff, and began to investigate the Army's nursing service. "I feel free for the first time in months," she told me.

But it was a hard kind of liberty. She could not avoid Carl Venning, or not entirely. Broome was too small for that. She might encounter him outside the bank in Carnarvon Street, loading cattle at the jetty, or drinking at the Continental, his boots propped up on the veranda rail in the twilight. Twice we saw him sitting alone in the cinema in Sheba Lane. He looked so ordinary. It was difficult for her to relate him to the man who had taken the Army major so seriously.

But, although Alice badly wanted to leave Broome behind her, she felt increasingly bound to it. First, the town was gearing up for a war in the Pacific. There was war talk wherever we cared to listen. A new meat works and a fish-curing works had been built to provide food for the wider war effort, and planes crowded the airstrip of the Royal Australian Air Force's new Advanced Operational Base. Young airmen and soldiers jostled us on the footpaths. I was their age, but they looked so much younger. We could not imagine them holding the country against an invader, but that was why they were there. As the weeks passed, Alice wondered if she was doing the right thing by leaving.

Then there was me, and my father, and Mitsy. I worried Alice because it was clear to everyone that for the rest of my life I would live with pain and always walk with a limp, my wasted leg swinging stiffly as I went along. "Who's going to make you exercise?" she demanded. "Who's going to massage your leg to keep it supple?" Our father worried her because he had lost all his old spirit. He couldn't sleep. We'd find him sitting in darkness sometimes, marked by the brief red eye of his cigarette. "Collecting my thoughts," he'd say. He kept the chandlery store open six days a week, to keep pace with the increased shipping in and out of Roebuck Bay, but he missed his old active life, even though it had ultimately been the source of his greatest guilt and sorrow.

But my father and I were not stones around Alice's neck. We were capable of caring for ourselves, and Alice knew that. All we needed was for something to come along and wake us up, and she couldn't do that for us. No, it was the loss of Mitsy's friendship that paralyzed her the most. "I wish I could patch things up with her," she told me one day, "then I could leave with a clear conscience."

•

It had long been a tradition in Broome to observe the Festival of the Lanterns. Although it was a Japanese festival, everyone gathered at the full moon in August each year and honored the dead. It was solemn but never depressing. I'd always found it fun. But this time we were honoring someone we knew and had been close to.

In 1941 the August full moon occurred a few days before my nineteenth birthday. The graveyard was illuminated by a cloudless moon, the tiny red specks of burning incense, and the paper lanterns in the trees. Japanese widows and children sat on the tombstones and murmured to the souls of the dead, who, it was said, had returned to earth when the sun settled into the sea and would stay and mingle with us until midnight. All the luggers were in. Massed flowers scented the air; drums rumbled; a knot of solemn girls swayed and dipped with fans; a sword dancer sliced the moon into flashing shards of silvery light about his head. We saw Mitsy and Sadako and they saw us, but we didn't speak, just nodded.

Later we sat and solemnly ate from overloaded trestle tables, before following the women, the children, and the lugger crews to the foreshore, where model boats were loaded with miniature lanterns, flower petals, and bundled food. We waited. When the tide turned and a soughing wind pulled at us from the sea, each little boat was launched into the water. When some sank — souls in strife — Alice and I watched the boat bearing Zeke. We could scarcely breathe. I found that I was trembling, willing him, willing him along. . . . And he glided, glided, glided, all the way out through Entrance Point, helped by Mitsy and Sadako, who beat tiny hammers against tiny bells and sang him sweetly to heaven.

The crowd dispersed then. I excused myself and limped to where I had last seen Mitsy. It was an intolerable situation, this unspoken standoff between our families, but more than anything, I wanted what I'd come to depend upon in my hospital bed, the sensation of Mitsy's healing hands on me, and of the electric flutter I'd felt in the pit of my stomach, that left me wide open and weak and breathless, wanting to be deep inside Mitsy, separate from her but melded to her. There aren't the words for conveying the nuances or contradictions of sexual desire. How can I tell you that I felt a greedy hunger for Mitsy's elastic bare skin, and relief and tenderness, and abdication of myself, all wrapped up in one? I wanted action, not buried thoughts.

I could make it happen, I decided. I saw a way to do it, a way of putting my foot in the door.

Mitsy and Sadako were talking to an old woman who had lost her husband in the cyclone of 1908, when 150 men were killed and many luggers lost to the deep. I kept well clear, but circled around so that Mitsy would notice me. The set of her face and her body in the fluttery light of the moon and the lanterns I can only describe as contained and striking. I couldn't take my eyes away from her. But if she noticed me, she gave no sign of it.

Then the old woman shuffled away and it was Sadako who spotted me there, waiting in the shadows. She beckoned to me.

Sadako didn't say anything but simply clasped my forearm tightly and looked up at me, before turning away to join another widow. Her face showed nothing but I was left with an impression of powerful feelings: sadness, but also relief, for no longer was Zeke lost and restless.

I turned to Mitsy. "Hello."

"Hello."

"Long time, no see."

It was a stupid thing to say, awkward and fumbling, and too pointed, like a criticism. I saw a flicker of annoyance on her face, before she said brightly, "How are you? How's the leg?"

"Getting stronger."

"That's good."

She was looking to escape me. I said rapidly, "Mitz, Alice is leaving Broome."

Some of Mitsy's energy drained away and she bowed her head. "I heard."

"She's been accepted as an Army nurse."

"She'll be needed, I suppose. Everybody knows the dreaded Japanese are poised to take over the world."

"Mitsy, that's not fair."

She stared stubbornly into the darkness.

"She wants to patch it up with you, Mitz. She misses you." I gave a high, false, jokey laugh. "In fact, *I* miss you, my *leg* misses you."

Mitsy swung around and said, "No one's stopping any of you from visiting us."

I thought my way through that. Mitsy's prohibitive manner *had* stopped us from visiting. But it was possible that she felt bad about that now, and was saying she wanted to be friends again. She'd put herself and her mother out in the cold, and wanted to come back inside.

"I'll tell Alice."

"Good."

We stared at the ground. "Did you know Jamie's training in Canada?"

Mitsy nodded. "He's coming back in November. His father pulled some strings to get him posted to Broome."

That surprised me. I'd had only one letter from Jamie, and he'd said nothing about his movements. "How do you know?"

"He writes to me," Mitsy said simply.

I stared at her, trying to read her expression. My mind churned. Jamie was supposed to be my friend, but he was telling Mitsy things, not me. And the old Jamie couldn't stand his father, and would never have let him pull strings on his behalf, so he must have pulled them himself, so that he could be close to Mitsy.

Was Mitsy pleased about that?

"Mitz," I said, "would you like to see a film sometime soon?"

"I don't think so, Hart, thanks for asking."

"I just thought —"

"My mother doesn't like to be alone. But why don't you visit? Tell Alice I'd love to see her again."

It was a cruel irony. I'd mended the breach between Alice and Mitsy, but it hadn't got me closer to her, which had been my main intention.

•

Alice felt more contented now, and saw Mitsy almost daily, as she waited for her travel orders to arrive. But whenever I was with them I sensed that there were things they could not talk about. They concentrated on the past, when we were children together. Sometimes Mitsy massaged my leg, but her strong hands had comfort rather than desire in them and she would talk across my supine body as she worked the wasted muscles, asking Alice to remember some mischief we'd got up to.

Alice got her travel orders in early November. It had long been our father's custom to celebrate birthdays, exam results, and anything at all with dinner on board the MV *Koolama* whenever she moored at the Broome jetty on her way north or south with provisions for the coastal towns. He'd be gravely formal with us, his shirt dazzling white under a dark jacket. I can remember the candles, the heavy cutlery on starched linen, and the faint spine-lurch from time to time as our chairs transmitted the scrape of the hull against the jetty. Even if the *Koolama's* broad beam happened to be squatting on the mud, awaiting a floating tide, I imagined movement in her bones.

This time on board we were saying good-bye to Alice. RAAF planes would be taking her in stages to Fremantle, where she would embark on a troopship bound for Malaya. The atmosphere was subdued. We didn't want Alice to go.

At one point my father said, "You asked Mitsy to come?"

"Yes."

He watched her face astutely. "But it's awkward for her, your going into the Army."

"Yes."

"She feels torn."

"Yes."

He nodded. "You might find yourself nursing blokes who've been wounded by the Japs."

Alice played with her fork. "Yes."

He was troubled. "We're her friends, but it must seem as if we're her enemies."

"Dad, she wasn't even born in Japan."

"It's not as simple as that."

Alice sighed. "I know."

The only other people dining on the *Koolama* were sedate

middle-aged couples and the town's civil servants. The young men of the district were at war or raising cattle and sheep for the war, and the young women were married or working in munitions factories down south.

And so Jamie Kilian stood out, a young man in uniform. He came in with his parents and two other couples — the police sergeant and the administrator of the leprosarium and their wives. When he saw us he waved and came over to our table. "I'm back," he said unnecessarily, grinning from ear to ear. He looked vivid and compelling.

"On leave?" said my father, who no longer seemed to know the town's gossip.

Jamie shook his head, still grinning. "Stationed here. They've got me flying Hudson bombers." He laughed. "The slowest crate in the sky."

He went back to his table, but later we were invited to join the Kilians. I was pleased to see Jamie again, but also wary. Why had he been writing to Mitsy? I watched while he joked with Alice about the latrines and numbskull officers that would soon be her lot in life. He wasn't being insufferable, but with his swagger and his youthfulness, his good fortune and his innocence, he was riding high in the world, as if he didn't expect to encounter trouble. If it happened, he'd laugh it off. Someone like that could be appealing, it occurred to me, if you were like Mitsy, grieving for your dead father. But Jamie was also in uniform, ready to go to war against the Japanese, and I wondered if she'd see him as the enemy.

When we got home that night, Saltwater Jack and Bernadette were hovering near the front door, waiting for us. They were very distressed.

"Derby," Bernadette sobbed. "They got Derby."

We couldn't get any sense out of her. My father took hold of Jack's arm. "Jack, listen, what's this about Derby?"

"They bin take that blackfella to jail, boss."

"Jail? What for?"

Jack was full of shame and delicate feelings, as though he didn't want Alice to hear him. I scarcely heard him myself. "Boss," he murmured, "Derby bin do something to a sheila and put her in the hospital."

Come to Grief

My *first instinct* was to conjure up a mental image of Derby Boxer and search for the violence in it, but all I could see in my mind's eye was a shy man who was scarred by hard work and liked to watch cowboy films.

My father took charge. First he telephoned the Continental, hoping that Carl Venning was still in Broome.

"Checked out," the night clerk told him. "Left two days ago."

I followed my father into the wireless room and watched him call Hartog Downs Station on the pedal transceiver radio. Venning answered. I stood there, listening to my father's side of the conversation and imagining the ghostly whispers and echoes on the line. The conversation went something like this: "Mike Penrose here, Carl. I thought you should know, the troopers have got your boy Derby in the lockup. . . . Yes, I know. . . . It's not our fault he gets stuck into the grog. . . . His sister doesn't drink. . . . Well, did you look for him first? . . . He could need bailing out. . . . Fine, if you're not going to do it, I will. . . . Tomorrow morning . . . Mate, he's your head stockman. . . . Attacked a girl apparently. . . . But what if he didn't do it? . . . Dump him, just like that? To hell with you."

My father flung down the headphones. "The bastard doesn't want to know. Just washes his hands of him. Says he's hired himself a new head stockman and Derby can go hang for all he cares."

There was nothing we could do that night, and the following morning we were due to take Alice to the Broome aerodrome. We might have stayed up talking, the three of us and Jack and Bernadette, but Derby's arrest and Carl Venning's indifference to it dampened our spirits and we were in bed by half-past ten. I lay there thinking. How much of Carl Venning's attitude was genuine, and how much was it spite, for being dumped by Alice?

The flight left at six. The sun was low at that hour, the tree shadows long across the airstrip, and my father and I shaded our eyes as we waited. Twice the takeoff was aborted when kangaroos wandered onto the strip. My father muttered, "Hurry up," from time to time. In part he was anxious to visit Derby in the lockup, but he also hated the prolongation of Alice's departure, and, I realized suddenly, he was eager to watch the takeoff.

Alice had boarded a ten-seater Lockheed Orion, a low-wing monoplane with a wooden frame, fabric-covered wings and fuselage, and retractable wheels. My father was struck by the little airliner's fast, shapely potential as it sat at the end of the airstrip, its motor snarling. "Isn't she a beauty?"

Finally the Lockheed was a speck on the horizon, and we drove to the jail. Derby wasn't there. He'd been taken to a holding cell at the courthouse and was due to appear before the magistrate.

My father and I went next door and sought out Kilian's office. It's true that bureaucrats tilt back their chairs and lace their fingers together behind their heads in the face of angry petitioners. The ceiling fan creaked above us. The papers on Mr. Kilian's desk lay exhausted from the humidity. Jamie was sitting in a cracked leather club chair.

"Look here, Kilian," my father said. "I want to vouch for Derby Boxer's good name."

Jamie's father shrugged. "All in good time, Mr. Penrose. Today I'm simply ascertaining if he has a case to answer."

On the MV *Koolama* the previous evening, my father and Jamie's father had been referring to each other by their first names. I turned to look at Jamie. He seemed tense, as if deadened by his father's personality again.

My father said, "I'm telling you here and now, Derby didn't do anything."

"He admitted it."

"I don't believe you."

"Even so —"

"Derby isn't a violent man."

"He'd been drinking. You know as well as I do that alcohol and the blackfellow don't mix."

"I've *seen* him when he's drunk. I used to help his sister drag him home after a night on the grog. He doesn't get wild with it. Quietly sozzled, if anything. Inclined to sleep."

Jamie's father tapped a small pile of crowded typewritten pages on his desk. "This is a record of his interview with Constable O'Neill. Your fellow admits that he beat the girl and had carnal knowledge of her. My hands are tied."

On our way out I said to Jamie, "Why aren't you at the base?"

"I'm on leave. I don't start until next week."

I saw him cringe as his father clamped an arm around his shoulders. "The lad's been in Canada for the past few months. He needs some time with his family."

When we were out of earshot my father snorted, "No one needs time with that family."

An hour later we were in the courtroom, listening from the public gallery. The prosecuting policeman began by summarizing the events. Apparently Derby had been camping with friends in a settlement on the southern outskirts of Broome. He'd been there for three days, waiting while Carl Venning attended to business. Derby and his friends were drinking heavily. A fifteen-year-old girl was assaulted and beaten into a coma from which she was not expected to recover, and Derby had been arrested for it.

The policeman, Constable O'Neill, read a record of the interview to the court:

CONSTABLE O'NEILL: It is my intention to interview you in relation to the assault on a girl named Kitty Lombadina Worms on the afternoon of November the tenth. Since anything you say can later be used in court, you are not obliged to answer any of my questions. Do you understand?

DERBY BOXER: I do.

O'NEILL: Constable Wickham will type both the questions and the answers. Do you also understand that?

BOXER: I do.

O'NEILL: Now, your full name is Derby Pallotine Boxer
and you are the head stockman on Hartog Downs
Station, on the Broome to Port Hedland road?

BOXER: That is correct.

O'NEILL: Are you acquainted with a girl named Kitty
Worms?

BOXER: I am.

O'NEILL: How well acquainted are you?

BOXER: We are quite well acquainted. I have been in
Miss Worms' company on a number of previous
occasions.

My father stiffened. He stood up and said, "Your wor-
ship, really, that's not Derby speaking. He doesn't use stan-
dard English."

Kilian said sharply, "Sir, I cannot permit interruptions.
Any more and I shall have you removed from the courtroom. Do you understand? Go on, Constable."

O'NEILL: How did you first meet Miss Worms?

BOXER: She was with friends of mine.

O'NEILL: Was she with these same friends on the
evening of the ninth?

BOXER: She was.

O'NEILL: What did you do that evening?

BOXER: We was on the grog.

O'NEILL: What were you drinking?

BOXER: Port wine.

O'NEILL: This was a party?

BOXER: You might say that.

O'NEILL: How long did the drinking last?

BOXER: Till we ran out of grog. Next day sometime.

O'NEILL: Were you with Miss Worms the next afternoon?

BOXER: I was.

O'NEILL: Did anything happen between you?

BOXER: I done her over.

O'NEILL: Please explain what you mean.

BOXER: I hit Kitty with a piece of wood and had carnal knowledge of her.

O'NEILL: At what time was this?

BOXER: Half-past three.

O'NEILL: In what manner did you hit Miss Worms?

BOXER: With a stabbing motion.

My father held his head and moaned, "No, no, no. They've put words in his mouth."

That was clear to me by now. I was hearing a well-educated Derby, not the stockman Derby who'd had only a basic education. The police had reworked Derby's answers in order to secure a conviction. Derby's admission, his repetitions and formal constructions, were contrived by Constable O'Neill. I am not claiming that O'Neill completely fabricated the confession. He probably believed that he had the real culprit in custody. I expect that Derby *did* confess, either to please O'Neill, or out of a lifetime's habit of gratuitously concurring with anything that a white suggested, especially if he couldn't comprehend it. But O'Neill *did* lead a vulnerable man through the stages of a false confession, and grant him a linguistic facility that he didn't possess. I think that if we had been present at the interview, we would have seen Derby's acquiescence, his passive and unwitting participation in the scene set for him by Constable O'Neill.

O'NEILL: Where did you strike her?

BOXER: At the end of the lane that runs behind the post office.

O'NEILL: I mean, where on her body?

BOXER: I struck her head.

O'NEILL: I have here a lugger's cleat. Is this the weapon you used?

BOXER: It is.

O'NEILL: Why did you hit her?

BOXER: She was eyeing off the other blokes.

O'NEILL: They were there when you hit her?

BOXER: They was all sleeping it off in the creek.

O'NEILL: Did you have carnal knowledge of Miss Worms before or after striking her?

BOXER: After.

O'NEILL: Did she attempt to resist you in any way?

BOXER: She was unconscious.

O'NEILL: How was Miss Worms dressed at the time of the assault?

BOXER: She wore a sleeveless white frock and bloomers.

O'NEILL: I show you now a pair of women's undergarments. Are these the bloomers you mentioned?

BOXER: Yes, they are.

O'NEILL: Can you explain why you assaulted Miss Worms?

BOXER: So she wouldn't go with the other blackfellas no more.

My father and I rocked in distress, for Kitty Worms and for Derby Boxer. My father got to his feet again. He was trembling. "None of this rings true."

"Sir, I shall have you removed from the courtroom if you persist in interrupting the King's proceedings."

"That's not Derby talking," my father insisted. "If you

knew him you'd know he speaks a kind of pidgin English. You've got him using words that even *I've* never used before."

I stood next to him, leaning on my cane. "And if Derby was so drunk," I said, "how can he remember things so clearly? The time, for example. The dress she was wearing."

That was enough for Kilian. He nodded to the troopers at the back of the room, and my father and I found ourselves manhandled out onto the street. I caught Jamie's eye as it happened. There was a complicated expression on his face, almost one of shame, but I didn't care. For the moment, I was happy to lump him together with his father.

Hugging the Ground

Then one day Derby Boxer appeared at our back door. Kitty Worms had awoken from her coma and identified one of her cousins as her assailant. If that had not been enough to convince Jamie's father, the publican of the Prince Regent came forward to say that he'd found Derby, passed out on a straw mattress, in a shed at the rear of his hotel at the time of the attack. He'd not been able to rouse him so he'd let him sleep it off.

My father didn't waste any time. Derby was clearly distressed at the thought of spending another minute in Broome, believing that he'd only come to grief again if he stayed. Carl Venning wouldn't take him back, so that left his tribal people. They'd look after him. And the timing was perfect: The Wet was about to start, and they'd be leaving Hartog Downs for their ceremonial country. We packed a case for Derby and a boxload of tinned food, tea, and sugar, and thirty minutes later left Broome in the black Nash.

We headed south for ten hours. It was a terrible journey, for there had been early rains. The heavy steering wheel wrenched at my father's thin wrists as we crossed the ruts and washaways, raising blisters on his palms. He worked the gears. His shoulders ached. There were stretches where the track gave way to whipping grasses and top-heavy trees, or the big car slipped over greasy stumps and sailed to the floorboards through flooded crossings. In places, the grass reached higher than the roofline, and all we had was the suggestion of a path through it. My father announced at one point that he'd turned his back on the sea, but the land was not much better. "Air travel, son, that's the future," he shouted. "If we were in a plane now we'd be floating above all this, following peaks, creekbeds, and roads, not hugging the ground like a snail."

We drove with handkerchiefs tied over our faces. I had pushed up the windscreen, to let in the air, but grass seeds rode the wind, tumbling behind the plowing radiator of the car. Soon our hair was matted with seeds, but we needed the air. We pushed on. When the muffler tore away, my father patched it back with wire, adding heat blisters to the friction blisters on his poor hands. When we rode onto a claypan at the far edge of Hartog Downs many hours later, guided by Derby, the car was popping like a tractor.

We'd come to a tribal settlement. There were about twenty people in the camp. Some of the women wore flour-bag shifts and the men loincloths, but most were dressed in cast-off dresses and trousers. One woman was very pregnant. They greeted Derby with shouts and grins, then gathered quietly with flourbags and empty tins when Derby told them that we'd brought food with us.

I leaned against the car while Derby and my father doled out the food. The pregnant woman flopped her forearm over her brows and stared at me. "What your name?"

I realized that I had the sun behind me and shifted around on my wasted leg. "Hartley."

She turned to the women behind her, spoke rapidly, then beamed at me. "Him good name," she said, retreating with her rations.

Derby explained: "If him be a boy, she call him Hartley."

I hoped he'd survive. We'd seen a child's grave half a mile back, a small mound topped with an ochered stick and a white rag.

As we were leaving, Derby clasped my father's hand, then mine. "You bin good peoples," he said. "You bin good to this old blackfella."

I didn't feel that there was much goodness in me.

Love and Its Discontents

It was an odd, edgy time. Chance was in the air in late 1941. All the world was breathless, and Broome was wound as tight as a spring. Seamen from coastal steamers were bringing back reports of submarine sightings, Japanese spotter planes had been seen in the north, and our ears sharpened whenever we heard a foreign accent. Meanwhile a telegram arrived from Alice. She was in Kuala Lumpur, just back from watching cricket at the Sultan's palace, she said, but what my father and I wanted to know was: *How safe are you?*

I also went a little mad. I began to follow Mitsy, imagining that she was meeting Jamie, or I limped down John Chi

Lane and leaned on my cane outside the boardinghouse where she lived. I stood watching Jamie from the shadows of the Pioneers' Cemetery at the foot of the old jetty as he wandered on the sand. It didn't occur to me to ask him what he was doing, or to confront Mitsy, or even to conceal myself. Curiously, I felt invisible, or barely visible, like a shadow cast by an obscured moon.

Love, and its discontents, were only one side of my coin. There was also my loss of faith. I looked at Jamie Kilian, so healthy and vital in his uniform, and realized that the future offered me nothing except another unproductive year, then another and another. I would never go pearling again, heavy work tired me, and none of the armed services wanted a man with a gammy leg. Such a man can't run if he's shot at. He can't depress a brake pedal, or dig a trench, or stand at attention, or any of a hundred other things, useful and pointless alike. There was fatigue, too, and anger, but more than anything, there was a sense of insufficiency, as niggling as a pebble in my shoe. And so I began to drift in life.

Dim the Moon

When I look back now, the eruption in our lives seems powerful and concentrated, but really it was made up of a series of smaller disturbances over a period of three months.

First there was the news on December 7 that Japan had attacked the American fleet moored at Pearl Harbor, in Hawaii. We heard about it on the 8th, when the Prime Minister announced that Australia was now at war with Japan. Later we learned that the Japanese had also attacked targets in Malaya, Singapore, and the Philippines, and on several Pacific islands. We were shocked by the extent and vigor of Japan's opening blows, but not surprised. It had seemed inevitable. But my father and I had a more personal stake than most people in

Broome: Alice was in one of the war zones. We pictured her, in a makeshift tent hospital under shrapnel-torn palm trees, tending to wounded soldiers and civilians, and we feared for her life.

That was the first thing. The second was that an order went out to intern the Japanese. In 1941 there were just over a thousand people registered as Japanese aliens in Australia. About half of them were engaged in the pearling industry in the northwest. I didn't know it then, but military intelligence and the security service had been watching Japanese civilians for years, noting the names and activities of those who might be spies. They'd been watching the Germans and the Italians, too, but only some Germans and Italians had been interned at the start of the war in Europe. The Japanese, it was felt, had not been absorbed into the local population to the extent that the Germans and the Italians had. Also, the government hadn't allowed naturalization or promoted assimilation of the Japanese. I suppose too that the Japanese were easily identifiable as aliens. Indeed, our next-door neighbor, a Chinese taxi driver, was beaten up one day when he was mistaken for a Japanese by visiting sailors.

The authorities acted swiftly on December 8, right around the country. In Broome, a hundred Japanese were arrested and taken to the jail, which was designed to hold only fifty prisoners. Eventually tents were erected within the perimeter walls as more and more were arrested.

My father and I witnessed one of the arrests. We were walking to the chandlery store — slowly, for my leg is always stiff in the mornings — and talking about the bombing of Pearl Harbor, when we noticed a police car outside Alf Okamura's cottage near the wharf. Armed soldiers were guarding the front door, and just as we were passing, Constable O'Neill came out, helping Alf and his wife with a couple of suitcases. Alf looked bewildered; his wife was sobbing. O'Neill himself appeared awkward and apologetic. "Sorry, Alf," he was saying, "it's orders, it's for your own protection."

My father stopped. O'Neill's face darkened: ever since Derby Boxer's committal hearing he'd had my father and me down as troublemakers. "There's nothing you can do here, Penrose."

My father ignored him. "What's up, Alf?"

Alf looked helplessly at O'Neill, who said, "Internment order."

"For Alf and Peggy? You're joking."

"For every Jap in the country, mate."

"Where?"

"In the local lockup, for the time being."

And so we walked on. My father didn't speak for several minutes, but then he began, walking a few paces, stopping to declaim loudly, walking on, stopping again. It was exhausting.

"Alf?" he demanded of the air. "Peggy? What harm could

they do anyone? What about Sadako? Mitsy? Can you see them signaling to Jap submarines? Or blowing up the jetty?"

He laughed harshly. "Maybe they think Sadako might send secret messages out to sea in her soy sauce bottles. Maybe they think she'll insinuate herself into our lives and corrode our will."

We walked on, stopped again. "*All* of the Japanese?" I said. "Where will they put them?"

My father gestured vaguely at the bulk of the continent behind us. "Oh, somewhere over in the east, shove 'em in with the Germans and the Italians, I suppose."

The water of Roebuck Bay was like a sheet of tin foil reflecting the blue sky. I could smell the mangroves and sea salt. I had an image of Sadako and Mitsy torn away from Broome and set down in some cold, damp, humorless place full of foreigners and strife, and I wanted to cry. Sadako was too old, too innocent, too bound to the dirt lanes of Broome for that, and Mitsy was the one I loved. Why not a kind of house arrest?

We opened the shop and tried to work, but by noon my father had worked himself into a state of great agitation. He was worried about Sadako and Mitsy, fed by his permanent guilt about Zeke. We put the closed sign on the door and walked through to Chinatown.

We didn't get that far. The whole town was astir. Japanese people had been emerging singly or in small family groups from the lanes and alleys of Chinatown all morning, carrying their belongings in sacks and baskets and carpetbags. They had formed in a quiet, patient cluster on Carnarvon Street, and many locals had gathered to stare at them. No one was abusive, just curious.

My father pushed through impatiently, looking for Sadako and Mitsy. I hobbled in his wake and found him talking to one of his old divers, Joe Suzuki.

"What's up, Joe?"

"Waiting for the constable, boss, all packed up."

"He's arrested you?"

Joe shrugged philosophically. "Bound to soon, boss."

My father stared past him at the entrance to John Chi Lane. I could see his jaw working, a sure sign that he was trying to make a decision. I sensed at once what it was — should we or shouldn't we see if Sadako and Mitsy were okay? If we walked down John Chi Lane now, free men, Europeans, would it be seen as flaunting our freedom and superiority?

The business with Derby Boxer, only a few weeks earlier, had awoken all of my father's old instincts for a challenge, and now he had a new cause. Without conferring with me, or waiting, he pushed through the crowd.

I followed. It was about one o'clock by this stage, the sun was directly above us. The air in Chinatown was muggy, scented, as heavy as soup. We saw one or two Malay and

Filipino faces behind insect screens, but otherwise John Chi Lane showed no signs of life.

Until we came to number 23, where Mitsy and Sadako lived. There was a soldier outside, a bayonet fixed to his rifle, anxiously marking time as he weighed up the seriousness of the argument that was raging inside the boardinghouse. The loudest voice was Mitsy's: *"I thought you were my friend!"*

Then, *"Doing your father's dirty work for him."*

And, *"Looking down on me, just because I'm Japanese."*

The soldier moved to stop us. "Shove off, sonny," my father said, pushing past him into the house.

"You can't go in there," the soldier bleated at me.

"So, shoot me in the back," I said, and I followed my father's sweat-darkened shirt into the Sennosukes' tiny living room.

Sadako was there, and a young policeman, and Jamie Kilian — and Mitsy, staging a standoff. She was sitting cross-legged on Zeke's steamer trunk. The batik cloth had been removed, revealing travelers' labels from Tokyo, Shanghai, Macao, Hong Kong, Batavia, Manila, and ports all around the Pacific. I'd always assumed that the Sennosukes used it for storing bed and table linen, but, judging by Mitsy's determined expression, it contained other things.

She flared up when she saw us. "Marvelous. Now it's four against two."

"Steady on, Mitz," my father said. He turned to Jamie and the policeman. "Are they under arrest?"

"No," the policeman said.

"Jamie, have you got any authority here?"

"The police are short-staffed. They've asked for military assistance."

"Doing your father's dirty work for him!" Mitsy shouted.

"What dirty work?"

Jamie looked shamefaced. "We have orders to search this place."

"That's right," said Mitsy derisively. "I've got a bomb hidden under me and a radio in my undies."

Jamie blushed. My father grinned at him. "Well, son? Has she?"

"Papers," said Jamie sullenly.

"Papers?"

"Documents, plans, drawings. Names and addresses."

"Sadako and Mitsy have all that?"

"No, Zeke did," Jamie said. "He was a well-known member of a secret organization."

"Secret, my bum," Mitsy said. "It was a social club. Everyone belonged. We looked out for one another."

"Your father was the secretary," Jamie said stubbornly. "We need to see his papers. Look," he said, turning to us one by one, working an expression of calm and reason on to his face, "I asked for this particular duty because I know Sadako and Mitsy. I didn't want strangers storming in here, wrecking everything, upsetting everyone."

"Too late! We are upset!"

"Well, I'm sorry about that."

"So you should be."

My father held up his hand. "So you're not arresting them."

"No. At least, not at this stage."

"Why not?"

Jamie said helplessly, "It's a mess. We've been ordered to intern everyone, but the jail's full, there are divers still at sea, and widows and children are not considered as dangerous as men."

"I'm not a child," Mitsy shouted. *"And how do you know I'm not dangerous?"*

She looked dangerous to me. I grinned at her. After a moment, she grinned back.

"You know what I mean," Jamie said.

"But a child is *exactly* how you've always treated me," Mitsy said. "I can see that now. Something exotic. A doll."

Jamie looked hurt. "That's not true, Mitsy."

My father had had enough. "Let's all be reasonable about this. Jamie, you say you're not interning them. Are you confiscating their property?"

"Only Zeke's papers."

"Mitz, sweetheart, what do you say? If you give this young man what he's come here for, he'll go away and leave you alone. Is that correct, Jamie?"

Jamie nodded curtly.

After a long moment, Mitsy clambered off the trunk. She gave Jamie a deep, mocking bow. "All yours, kind sir."

Jamie blushed. "Thank you."

He opened the trunk. There were towels on top, then sheets and pillowcases, then tablecloths, napkins, a stack of bamboo place mats, and finally half a dozen of Sadako's ceremonial kimonos.

No papers of any kind.

"Mitz?"

There was a look of satisfaction on Mitsy's face. "Your spies have let you down, Jamie boy. My father's dead, or haven't you noticed? The club has a new secretary. We passed all Dad's papers on to him."

When Jamie and the policeman had left, Sadako asked us to stay. She put a warning finger to Mitsy's lips when Mitsy remonstrated, saying, "Daughter, these our friends." We four sat in the little room and sipped tea, and slowly mended a little of the rift that had developed between us.

Mitsy was quieter. She also seemed deeply tired suddenly, her features drawn and full of strain. "What will happen now?"

"Hart and I will intercede on your behalf," my father

replied. "We'll vouch for you. We'll see the magistrate this afternoon and ask him not to intern either of you."

Mitsy looked fully at both of us. "Thank you."

Jamie Kilian was finished, that much was clear. My voice was wobbly: "If anything happens, fetch us straightaway."

Mitsy nodded. Sadako bowed us out of the house.

•

A week went by. My father and I had two icily polite meetings with Jamie's father, and he finally agreed that Sadako and Mitsy would not be interned — "in the foreseeable future."

No one back then claimed to understand the fine print on the government's legislation. The authorities themselves had difficulty in deciding upon degrees of "Japaneseness," and who should be counted as a security risk and who was at risk from civilian reprisals. They interned single women, old men, children. They interned European and Aboriginal wives of Japanese-born men, mixed-race children, Australian-born Japanese. Many had never been to Japan. Some spoke only English, others only Japanese. Some Japanese were not interned at all, others were later released, and a few were not interned until well into 1942.

But the fact of the internment did isolate the Japanese of Broome. They were marked people now, aliens in our midst. Jimmy Ogawa's laundry business was ransacked, even though he'd been born in Broome and had an Aboriginal mother. Someone firebombed Kit Tsutsumi's photographic studio. Children were taunted at school.

Mitsy and Sadako were not immune. I visited them every day and heard how difficult their lives had become. "People spit on us in the street," Mitsy said. "They proposition us as if we were prostitutes."

Then came a day when I saw boards over the street-front windows. Sadako was seated on a cane chair, trembling, staring at the floor. "Someone threw rocks," Mitsy said. "Last night when we were asleep." She was clutching her arms across her chest. "Now the landlord wants us to get out." She glanced at me. "And Jamie Kilian's been around. Says he's looking out for our interests, but I don't trust him."

I went home and told my father. "They'll be safer with us," he said.

We made two trips in the Nash. First we collected Sadako and Mitsy, who brought their clothing and other belongings stuffed into cases and pillowslips. We showed them to adjoining rooms at the side of the house. One had been Ida's sewing room, the other was a spare bedroom. Both had a single bed, a chair, and cupboard space. Sadako was full of emotion. I saw her touch her palms together and say, in the doorway of the spare room, "Such a fine room."

"You'll be safe here," my father said.

"I cook, clean," Sadako said.

My father put his hand over hers. "That would be grand."

Then we went back for the steamer trunk, a couple of rice-paper screens and paper lanterns, and a set of cane chairs. When we returned home, we saw that Sadako had started decorating her room. She'd ranged six jade horses on the mantelpiece. At the center of them was a tiny wooden model of the *Ida Penrose,* painted with Japanese characters. I asked Mitsy later what the words meant. She was standing very close to me, so close that I could feel a tingling along my forearm. "A prayer," she said, "directing my father to heaven."

She reached up suddenly and pulled my head down. She kissed me. I reached out to touch her arm, but she was gone, slipping into her own room.

I found it difficult to fall asleep that night, and the next. I began to prowl the house at the deepest hours before dawn. Once I stood in Mitsy's doorway for some time. My leg ached. I returned to my room and tried to sleep.

Then, from the foot of my bed, Mitsy murmured, "Hart?"

She was a dark shape against the window, dimming the light of the moon. I opened my arms.

Angles and Hollows

I knew nothing about making love. Mitsy taught me how. Neither of us was experienced, but Mitsy had an instinct for it — or, rather, she knew that I was too feverish, too frantic, so that it was over too quickly, denying both of us the slow pleasures. She made us spend time simply embracing and stroking first, and it was far better that way. She was full of angles and hollows. I traced with my fingers the sharp bones of her rib cage and her spine, and watched the tendons flexing under her brown skin. I liked to taste her. She made me laugh. We discovered that my stomach at the start, before we'd scarcely touched, was so sensitive and so expectant, that the first flick of her fingers sent a shot of electricity through me. When she was ready, she coiled and uncoiled. I scratched her back afterward, long, slow scratching strokes, and that was her electric charge. My leg didn't horrify her. She made it part of the lovemaking. She liked its knobbiness, its carven ridges and dead tissue. Under her fingers, it tingled. It was a normal leg. Finally, we talked. Mitsy taught me how to lie with her and talk through the night. I've never been so close to anyone. How could you not be, when you start like that?

After that first time, we found a spotting of blood. Mitsy was overcome to see it. She smiled broadly at me, then bundled the sheets into her arms and took them to the laundry. It was six in the morning: the house was silent. We had just reached a milepost in our lives, and no one knew it.

There was no more blood, but we were nightly lovers, and very active, and so we were often scrubbing sheets and winding them through the wringer like lumpy pastry dough, and hanging them out to dry. We always washed shirts and underwear with the sheets, to convey our innocent intentions, but we probably needn't have bothered. Neither Sadako nor my father noticed anything.

Perhaps they did notice, and were either giving us their blessings or didn't know how to stop us. How could they not have known, unless they were more lost to their separate heartaches than concerned about us? Maybe they loved us because we were lovers. With the world outside going insane, did Mitsy and I represent something good and innocent? I don't know. Perhaps, simply, they were blind.

●

When I was outside the house, in the damp heat, Mitsy retreated, became a dream in my head. She inhabited the dark hours and the filtered moonlight. She never left the house and so when I wandered the streets and beaches and waterfront laneways, there was only me, daydreaming. I could not point to a street corner, palm tree, or rusty iron fence and say, "This is where Mitsy said she loved me," or "That's where Mitsy and I scratched our initials inside a heart."

On December 18 I was at the jetty when the remaining luggers docked at Broome. A crowd of us, with nothing better to do, gathered to watch the arrests. We saw Constable O'Neill take the Japanese divers one by one and put them onto an Army truck. They were bewildered. There were soldiers pointing guns at them and a half-curious, half-antagonistic crowd looking on, so who could blame them? By December 21, 185 Japanese had been interned.

"If you've got nothing better to do," Mitsy told me, two days later, "then you can help me in the kitchen tomorrow."

And so it was that I learned how to cook rice, brew Japanese tea, and make marinated fish and vegetable dishes.

At noon, Mitsy and I loaded the Nash and delivered everything to the jail. It was Christmas Eve and the internees were inclined to be festive, even though most of them were not Christian. The prison officers were easygoing about it. They said that we could visit the jail whenever we liked and they had even been allowing some of the internees to visit their wives and children at home from time to time.

After that, Mitsy left the house every day, but never to wander around Broome with me. She delivered food to the jail, ran messages between the jail and Chinatown, and lobbied the magistrate and the prison officers on welfare matters for the internees.

"Don't stir them up too much," I said, "or they'll lock you away."

We were still in love. She hugged me tightly and said, "Don't be such a stick in the mud. Besides, Jamie said that Mum and I won't be interned."

I struggled away from her, hurt. "You're seeing him too?"

"Relax. I went to see his father and happened to run into him, that's all."

On New Year's Eve she took me to the jail to help the internees celebrate. We ate special food prepared by Sadako, talked and sang, and later played card games. Here and there I saw tiny photographs of a uniformed Japanese man on display. "The Emperor," Mitsy whispered. "Don't tell anybody or we'll be in trouble."

We, she said. She seemed to see herself as an internee too, even though she was outside the wall. I began to recognize two different Mitsys: one the agitator and one the lover.

Of course it didn't go unnoticed that my father and I had given sanctuary to Mitsy and Sadako. As the war news worsened in the early days of 1942, people began to mutter whenever I passed them in the street. One of them even called out to me: "Hey, Penrose, I hear you're running a brothel. Got a pair of Jap whores."

Jamie came to the house a couple of times. He wanted to see Mitsy. He was out of uniform and coming as an old friend to both of us, he said. "Things are different now," I said. He turned away. I shut the door. I didn't tell Mitsy.

Rule of Darkness

The shift seemed sudden, but it must have been gradual, over a period of weeks. The first sign was an edginess in my father, who dug an air-raid shelter in the backyard and began to hang about our front gate like a wraith, waiting for the postman, waiting for news from Alice.

Waiting for news of a loved one . . . It's a condition encouraged by the unreality of war. Letter time is ordered differently from real time. It's rarely linear and responsive. Despite the regularity of the correspondence, some letters will fail to arrive, and others will arrive out of sequence or after weeks of silence. An anxious query might be met by an apology, a declaration by a reproval. An old letter, reread, might alter in meaning from one day to the next. And if there is a gap in the correspondence, you tend to read it as a deliberate silence, a rebuff. You chafe, needing to get at the truth. You lean your nose to the most recent letters as if all of the things that are lost or hidden might swim into view.

In worrying about Alice, my father felt all of these things, almost as a lover might. He sank into himself, and began to mutter about "Japs." If the wireless or the newspapers reported a lack of air support for the Allied troops in Malaya, he wondered aloud where Alice was. He traced skirmishes and battles on the maps published in the newspapers and trembled at the pace and scope of the Japanese advance. When the first of Broome's Japanese internees were finally placed aboard a ship that sailed for Fremantle, he seemed satisfied, not saddened, as he might have been six weeks earlier.

I suppose that I was more fatalistic. If Alice was dead, or about to die, or if the mail ships were being sunk, then there was nothing I could do about it. Or rather, I felt powerless, and guilty for loving Mitsy so much when the world was in such a mess.

Finally, Kuala Lumpur was abandoned to the Japanese. Airfields were bombed and shipping torpedoed. The Allies could not hold. By the end of January 1942, they were ready to cross the Causeway to Singapore, as civilians had been doing for six weeks, even as bombers raided the island.

Rabaul fell on January 23, Ambon on February 2. Then Malaya was lost to the Japanese, and we knew that Singapore, congested and barely fortified, was bound to be next.

Where was Alice?

Clearly, the Japanese did not have weak eyesight. Their planes were not constructed of bamboo and rice paper. Their weapons were reliable and their war machine was efficient. In Broome we scanned the skies, stocked our air-raid shelters, and oiled our rifles.

And, every evening after the news, we listened to the Department of Information broadcast.

I can still recall the uninflected, well-bred voice (a tweed coat and pipe-in-the-corner-of-the-mouth kind of voice), the darkness outside the window, the tea drawing in the pot, the windows masked with black bituminous paper, the wireless set on the shelf, and the scratchy hatred:

> *The Japanese violate our deepest and most fundamental instincts. The principle of White Australia shall never be overturned by armed aggression. An enemy setting foot on Australian soil will find himself up against a manhood of unparalleled strength and determination. Australia shall remain forever the home of a people whose descendants came here, to southern waters, in peace and established an outpost of the British race.*

> *There are some who continue to believe that the*
> *Japanese are pleasant at heart, content to breed goldfish*
> *and grow chrysanthemums. They believe only a minority*
> *are capable of barbarism, and that Japan is the most in-*
> *dustrious and progressive nation in Asia.*
>
> *These are the delusional and ill-informed beliefs of*
> *the appeaser. Japan is not interested in peaceful co-*
> *existence with Australia. We are too valuable to them for*
> *that. In fact they hate us, vilely and savagely. But we do not*
> *hate. We find the Japanese too loathsome for hatred, and*
> *shall not rest until they have been cleared from the earth.*

We listened, the war news worsened, no letters came, and the hatred poured from the wireless night after night. I suppose it's only natural that we should be touched by it. My father rarely went down to the chandlery store now. He stayed indoors, and, before long, had begun to watch Mitsy and Sadako suspiciously whenever they passed him in the house. He'd listen to the radio every evening and swivel about in his armchair as though he sensed them standing in the shadows behind him — two lithe killers, not an old woman from Broome and her daughter.

Nothing was done and nothing was threatened, but Mitsy's and Sadako's presence in the house became a confusing element in my relationships with them. I felt allied to my father, to the memory of my sister, to my lover, to my lover's mother. Couldn't I love them equally, and not take sides? We grew uncomfortable with one another.

The evenings were very long. We tried to make them more pleasant. My father played the gramophone as a break from the wireless, and I read, or talked to Mitsy, but Sadako stayed in her room. When Mitsy turned nineteen, we had a party. We couldn't manage to encourage much good cheer. Alice was always there, that's what it was — in our heads, in the corners of every room. Was she dead? Why hadn't we heard anything? We suffered from a kind of paralysis. We wanted news from her more than we wanted to do something about the tension in the house, and so we did nothing but wait.

The days passed. Late on February 15 we heard that Singapore had fallen to the Japanese. Very few people had escaped. The next afternoon a small silver airliner circled over the town before heading for the aerodrome. It bore Dutch markings, an inverted orange triangle on the tail and wings. I recognized it as a Lockheed Lodestar, and heard that it had come from Batavia. The Japanese were coming, and so the Dutch were getting out of Java.

What's so painful to me about this time, as Singapore fell and Java waited, is my treachery. Mitsy and Sadako began to look less benign. Of course they changed only in my perceptions of them, not in fact, but perception is everything. They seemed to undergo a kind of shape-shifting. It was as if they'd been caught in the tricky, variable light and shadow of a candle — only the alteration was permanent, not momentary. Darkness ruled the world. I felt eyes at my back.

How can you love and hate someone at the same time? How can you continue to want them, and yet despise them? It has happened to all of us, but when it first happens there is nothing more hurtful and confusing. We feel bad. We act badly. We are not ourselves, or are the worst of ourselves, the side we're scarcely aware of.

For a time, Mitsy continued to slip into my room every night. We continued to make love, right under the eyes of a world that was bound to disapprove. In a sense, we were making love to forget, or to push the badness aside until daylight broke.

But, as I said, Mitsy seemed to alter. We'd make love, and immediately afterward all my tenderness and desire would drain away. I'd not want her to stay the night. It was a short step from that to having hateful sex with her. One night she didn't come to my room at all.

And yet I continued to want her. She filled my head. I thought that if I could cure the hatefulness in me we could love again. She avoided me. She would shut herself away with Sadako or pass by me mutely in the rooms and corridors. When she went out — always at night, now — I followed her.

This was an echo of that bad time before the war. Mitsy led me straight to Jamie Kilian. Of course, they could not meet in his barracks at the RAAF aerodrome, or at his father's house, or in the street in broad daylight, but only where secret lovers meet. I followed them to the beach, to parkland, to shadowy lanes, and to the wind-shaped rocks at Ganthaume Point. Their kisses were quick and chaste. They touched hands only briefly, before sitting or strolling. They seemed like nothing more or less than friends, in other words, but I knew better.

Soundings and Sightings

Then, one morning, a letter came. It was from Malaya, but my father's name and address were typed, not handwritten. I think my father began to fracture and break even then, before he'd opened it. He boiled the kettle, brewed the tea, carried the cup and saucer and a plate of biscuits out onto the back step, poured the tea, and tore open the envelope. I saw him lift his teacup with one hand, then smooth the letter over his knee with the other.

For a moment, I wondered if he'd hunched over to sneeze. A gout of black tea splashed over his wrist; I waited for the curse, the burning flick of his fingers. Instead, his head snapped back, and a long, triggering spasm poured through him. He began to topple. His legs straightened like rams and I heard the juddery scrape of his boot heels on the concrete. My father's decline was like an unfolding story. I followed it, episode by episode. It was not until the cup shattered and he'd stabbed a hand through the rotting fly-screen that I had witnesses.

Sadako rushed past me from the kitchen. She crouched at the screen door, pushed at it experimentally. "Mr. Penrose-*san?*"

I watched. My father was lodged heavily against the door, pinning it shut. Mitsy's face materialized in front of me. "Hart? Don't just stand there, help us."

I blinked. "We'll go out the front door and around the side of the house."

We freed my father from the screen door, and together we dragged him through to the sitting room and stretched him out on his back. Mitsy and Sadako crouched over him. While Mitsy mopped his face with a washcloth, Sadako slipped off his boots, unbuttoned his shirt, and removed his belt and braces. I watched her fingers move down his body. My father was composed of warm cotton, pliant skin, and secret odors. She seemed to linger over him, as if he reminded her of Zeke. She kept her face averted. Perhaps I imagined it. Or perhaps she hungered to lay her hands on ordinary human skin and warmth.

"The letter," I said.

Mitsy rested on her heels and lifted my father's left hand into her lap. Slowly she peeled open his fingers. I saw the resistance, the stiff articulation of his knuckle joints. The letter, wadded as tight as a handkerchief, seemed to sigh and swell on contact with the air. Mitsy handed it to me.

I scanned it first. It was an official letter from Alice's commanding officer, and had taken eight weeks to reach us. Apparently Alice had been with a dozen other nurses and a number of wounded soldiers on board a little hospital ship in the Straits of Malacca when it was attacked by Japanese fighter planes. The presence of the fighters had made rescue difficult. Some bodies were pulled from the water later, but Alice was not amongst them, and so she'd been reported officially as missing. I didn't overlook the irony: just days after we had offered sanctuary to Sadako and Mitsy, Japanese fighter pilots had been shooting at Alice. I felt my face twist. I felt a spurt of burning tears, and said to Mitsy, "You bitch."

I'm trying now to step into Mitsy's skin. She has my father's head in her lap and knows, from her nursing, that half of his body has been paralyzed by a stroke. Her mother is nearby, but it's not her mother who has her attention but me, a crying boy, my face red and wet and hate-twisted. I had been the one she loved and I had let her down. I had not listened to my heart but to the mutter of the war. She snatches the letter from me, sees at a glance what it says, and swings back her hand and slaps me left and right across the face.

I remember that everything collapsed inside me. "Sorry," I said. "Sorry."

"Hart," she said evenly, "we need to get your father to the hospital."

I nodded. I got up. Together we carried him out to the Nash and bundled him onto the backseat.

"I won't be coming with you, Hart."

Again I nodded. I started the car, backed it out, and took my father to the hospital.

•

I waited through the long day. At one point there was a commotion when a jeep fishtailed to a halt in the dirt outside the emergency doors and two Dutch airmen staggered in, supporting a pregnant woman whom they said had gone into labor. They had just landed their Dornier flying-boat in Roebuck Bay. The contractions, they said, had started a couple of hours after takeoff from Java. "We were attacked in the air," they told me. The date was February 19. A few hours later we heard that the Japanese had bombed Darwin that day. I suppose a stray fighter or reconnaissance plane had spotted the Dornier on its way back to base after the raid.

At five in the afternoon the doctor told me to go home.

"We'll keep your father here for a few days," he said. "I'm sure he'll get most of his speech and movement back."

That night I wanted Mitsy. I wanted to be loved and for things to be made better in my head. I went to her room. She wasn't there.

•

The days passed. It was at about this time that I found my father's logbooks. I'd been searching for his box of service medals and the photographs he'd taken in Palestine during the Great War, when I happened to look under his bed. A dozen ship's logs were stacked there. I hauled them out.

They were, in fact, diaries, a record of his turbulent soul. He'd recorded wind velocities, soundings, sightings, and daily summaries, like any sailor, but he'd also written: *Ida and I were kissing, and something made me open my eyes. Hers were already open, staring at me like I was a specimen. . . . I can't hold on to her much longer. . . . I'm a plain man and I've led a plain life, but it doesn't follow that I'm a man of plain feelings, does it? I burn for her. If only she knew how I felt. . . . I followed her for three days, but it wasn't what I thought. It turns out she wasn't meeting Anderson at all, but going down to Ganthaume Point with a book, shutting herself off like she needed a rest from us. . . . I look at Alice and Hartley sometimes and I could weep, I feel so strongly about them. . . .*

I read through each logbook, an excited, confused, and troubled spy, then shoved them back where I'd found them.

There was one empty logbook. I kept it. I liked the smell and the texture of the leather binding and the thought of crisp pen strokes on the stiff pages. I began to write in it, to express myself and to mark the paper. In one sense, the logbook was a substitute for Mitsy. It gave me emotional comfort. The scratching-pen sensation was physically satisfying. I wrote to find a perspective on the things that troubled me, to reshape my life, to record the progress of the healing of my leg, to heal myself. But to keep a journal is to take the short view. Today, working from memory and those journal entries, I'm taking the long view, and it's liberating.

Sometimes I recorded bald facts. I wrote that Darwin had been bombed but neither the newspapers nor the wireless were revealing much about the raids. I wrote that all the women and children of Broome were evacuated soon afterward. But mostly I wrote what I felt. My entry for the first of March 1942, for example, reads: *I feel increasingly trapped in Broome. I hate the proximity of the water and yet I feel fixed too firmly to the ground, the way I press upon it so heavily, leaving marks in the dirt. I'd like to be Jamie. I'd like to fly.*

Pity and a kind of shame lodged in me when I read that my father had followed my mother, afraid of what she might be doing, too afraid to inquire. I saw myself in him and was mortified.

I stopped following Mitsy, but I needed a distraction and found it in the harbor. Broome had become a refueling stop in the evacuation of Java, and the busiest port in the northwest. Eight thousand Dutch civilians, colonial officials, and senior military types passed through the town in the last two weeks of February. Planes of the Royal Netherlands Army and Navy, Qantas, and the RAAF shuttled them over the Torres Strait to Broome, a distance of 560 miles, where they landed and refueled for the final stage south to Perth, or they dropped their passengers in Broome and turned back for another load. On one day alone, fifty-seven aircraft passed through. One pilot went for more than eighty hours without sleep. As soon as he'd landed his passengers and refueled, he'd fly back to Java to collect more.

It was a desperate, fearful time, and it meant that Broome was full of strangers. The flying-boat passengers slept on board their aircraft moored in the bay, but food and shelter had to be found for those who'd landed at the aerodrome in bombers and airliners. The hotels, the school, and many private homes were full. A shuttle service to Port Hedland was set up to relieve the strain. Jamie Kilian took part in it, and he also ferried women and children to Perth, together with the old, the sick, and the wounded.

I liked to limp down in the mornings for a couple of hours before visiting the hospital, and simply watch. It was a world full of little stories — an airman sunning himself on the vast wing of a Catalina; the arguments that flared between tired and anxious people; the Dutch child with a cat she'd smuggled aboard a Dornier flying-boat; the refueling lighter *Nicol Bay* colliding with a drifting lugger; pilots coming to shore in rowboats to sign papers and beg for fuel. One morning a Dutch plantation owner said to me, "The Germans have overrun Holland, the Japanese have overrun Java — where can I go, now?" I saw a Dutch woman scream at Gideon, an old Filipino who had once worked the pearling fleets as a deckhand, for refusing to go into town to buy her a bag of fruit. To her, he was just a native. She had spent all her life relying on native servants and now the edifices of her existence were collapsing around her.

The Broome jetty is half a mile long. I'd limp out to the end, counting the Empire, Catalina, and Dornier flying-boats. The Dorniers wore Dutch markings, the Catalinas American, Australian, or English markings, and the Empires belonged to Qantas. I liked the Dorniers. They crouched in the water like clumsy dragonflies, the long main wing on a series of struts above the fuselage, three motors in a row.

And every evening I'd walk to a high point in the town and look out over the bay. We were twin cities, twinkling with lights, a new city on the water and the old one with its back to the desert.

The Divine Wind

On the morning of March 3, I counted five Dorniers, eight Catalinas, and two Empire flying-boats moored in the bay, about half a mile out from the sea end of the jetty. They were full of Dutch civilians. Some, who were sitting on the wings, enjoying the early sun and the sea air, waved to me.

I limped back. I thought about opening the shop, but what did we have there that a flying-boat captain could need? It was a humid day. There was always the threat of rain and cyclonic winds in March. I found shelter under a palm tree and rested my leg. The Qantas Airways agent was sitting there too, smoking agitatedly, snatching the cigarette from his mouth to mutter at me.

"Don't like it, sonny."

"Don't like what?"

He gestured at the flying-boats. "Look at them, sitting ducks. What time is it?" He looked at his watch. "Nine o'clock and they're all refueled, ready to go, but no, have another cup of tea, a fag, a snooze in the sun. Sitting ducks."

"Sitting ducks for what?"

He stared at me. "Where have you been lately? Three o'clock yesterday, along comes this Jap spotter plane, makes three circuits of the harbor. This morning, about four o'clock, another plane comes over. They even reckon someone was signaling to it with a torch."

He glanced at me sourly. "I hope you're keeping an eye on them Japs you got up at your house, sonny." He looked away again. "Something big's going to happen. I can feel it in my bones."

I was spooked by him, and offended. I hauled myself upright and hurried back to the house.

There was an Air Force jeep parked in the driveway. I'd been gone for only thirty minutes. They wouldn't have been expecting me to come back for hours.

Mitsy's and Sadako's belongings sat neatly inside the front door.

I went through to the kitchen and found Jamie and

Mitsy hovering anxiously while Sadako packed a box with rice cakes and a flask of green tea.

"You bastard, Kilian."

Jamie turned. "Hart, it's not —"

I rode over him. "Your old man said they wouldn't be interned."

"Circumstances —"

Mitsy cut him off. "Hart, listen, we —"

"No warning at all," I said.

I don't often feel anger. I almost never show it. But sometimes it comes flooding into me out of nowhere and I can't control it. I frighten people when it happens. I can almost visualize it, a swamping wave of badness, filling me from my guts to my brain in less than a second. It's as if my skull will crack open.

I launched myself at Jamie, swinging my fists at him. Have you ever heard the sickening bone-slap of a heavy punch to the jaw? Jamie's head snapped back. Blood spurted from his nose. He shook himself and blinked, then rather than step away, closed the distance and grappled with me. We knocked a chair over. We swung around and Sadako and Mitsy dodged away from us, calling out to us to stop. It was an exhausting, futile, scrabbling, inexpert fight that ended when we overbalanced and pitched onto our knees. My leg was shot through with pain.

In the aftermath, as we gasped and the women watched us, disappointed and afraid, I heard the stutter of heavy machine guns. A plane snarled away over the house, then returned.

We hurried outside. I counted them, two, four, six fighters, silvery in the blue sky, with the red rising-sun roundels of Japan on the wings and fuselage. They had just finished strafing the flying-boats in the bay and were banking for a second run. They came in low and fast, at no more than five hundred feet, firing shells and tracers. I imagined them, up above the world, confident and powerful, sweeping everything before them, like a divine wind.

Jamie swung around, tracking a more distant formation of fighters. "They're attacking the field!" He ran to the jeep, showering us with shellgrit as he sped away.

Sadako began to weep. She tucked her chin into her chest and folded her arms over her head and rocked and wailed.

"Hush," Mitsy said. "Hart, help me take her into the shelter."

Down into the damp earth, where the air smelled of swampland and mold. Twice during the Wet my father had had to pump the water out. We sat Sadako on a folding chair, a broken figure in the gloom, and I was about to unfold another for Mitsy when she snatched it from me and tossed it aside.

"We need to get down to the harbor. There'll be people in the water, people dying."

Again the chatter of the guns and the Japanese fighters peeling away, climbing, turning for another strafing run. It was a strangely quiet battle, with little sense of urgency about it. We could not see the damage, only the six little specks in the dome of the sky. We could hear the machine guns and the diving scream of aero engines, but at a distance. There was no ground resistance, apart from a tiny useless popping sound that might have been a rifle. If this was an invasion, it seemed to me small and pointless.

Until I reached the harbor. Suddenly the war was large and very real. Those hadn't been silver insects in the sky but death dealers. They came in again, southwest this time, hard and fast over our heads, holding out until the last second before firing. I saw a sudden stitching of holes in the fuselage of a Catalina. It settled deeper into the water, leaking fuel. Other planes were burning. The sea was alight. I saw a black figure in the water raise a smoking arm. The flesh was gone from its fingers.

"Dad's dinghy," I said.

It was kept on the sand, well clear of the jetty, in among other dinghies and rotting hulls and empty drums and rusty anchors. Mitsy helped me down and we stumbled across the sand, keeping low. On the jetty the harbormaster was firing a rifle. The *Nicol Bay* came in, loaded with people plucked from the sea. I saw the Qantas agent farther around the bay, straining on the mooring rope of a beached rowboat.

As Mitsy and I pulled away from the beach, into the oily water and the storming fires and screams, the attack planes came in from the seaward end of the bay, firing at the fuel drums on the jetty. I seemed to find my sense of smell suddenly, as though it had been lost to me. I could smell aviation fuel and oily smoke and, almost, almost, charred meat. These things tasted in my mouth. My senses ran together in pity and fear, and I pulled so hard on the oars that the little boat changed direction and Mitsy had to clutch the sides and shout a warning at me.

It was a dinghy designed for four people. That first trip we plucked twelve from the water. Seven rode inside, while the others swam with us, one hand on the boat, kicking their legs. We were slow and heavy and low in the water, and fearful of sharks. We spotted a Dutch officer floating on his back. He had a baby girl stretched out on his chest, her little head lifting clear of the water, eyes huge in her skull, looking about in wonderment. I snatched her to safety. The Dutchman seemed to sigh, roll over, and die in the water.

As we came in, I saw Jamie arrive in his jeep. He ran to

the sand, pulled another dinghy into the water. Then I forgot about him.

Three of our passengers had burns and one had been cut by glass. Mitsy stayed with them on the sand and called to the harbormaster for a medical kit. "You must be joking," he said. "You and your tricks."

I grabbed him. "Don't be so stupid. She's a nurse. She's lived here all her life, you useless bastard."

He rolled his eyes at me but gave Mitsy the medical kit, and she began to treat the wounded.

I set out again. The sharks had come in. They'd tasted the blood and sensed the fear in the thrashing limbs. I saw a boy gasp and open his mouth, then drop beneath the surface as if pulled down by a stone. The water boiled above him. I dragged people onto the dinghy, headed for shore, helped Mitsy, went out again.

Later I found myself in a patch of oil. The sea licked dreamily at the bow of the dinghy, streaking it. In the light of the sun and the flames, the oil glistened like mother-of-pearl, like spilled paint of many colors. Then it began to burn. There were two people in there. One was dead. The other croaked, "Hart."

It was Jamie Kilian. A curious sort of peace settled in me. There was no urgency, no war, no need to pluck and flee. I gazed at him. I could let him die. I could let him drown or burn or be tugged beneath the deep by a man-eater. His hand rose, dripping, and I took it.

That oil. It was like grabbing a bar of soap. The dinghy swung away. His hand slid from my grasp. Behind him the dead man was alight in the water.

To reach Jamie I had to straddle the side of the boat. I lay along the gunwale, my bad leg trailing in the water, and reached my hand to him. The boat tipped and swung again and I missed. I scooped the water. Jamie's uniform was bunched at his neck. When the boat came around again, I grabbed for his collar, not his hand, and hauled him in.

"Your leg."

I was burning. Some of the scars I have now are from that fire, the burning water of Roebuck Bay on March 3, 1942. I didn't feel anything at the time. I stripped my trousers off and dumped them into the sea.

Jamie closed his eyes in exhaustion. He was quiet. I began to row.

"What happened?"

His eyes snapped open. "The base was all shot up. Every plane destroyed, an American bomber shot down. There was nothing I could do, so I came here. I took a dinghy out —"

"I saw you."

He nodded. "The planks were rotten. It began to sink."

I rowed. Jamie began to cough; he'd swallowed oil. After a while he said, "You were going to let me die."

"No."

"Just for a moment, Hart. It was there in your eyes."

The thing about close relationships is that you fall into old patterns no matter what the circumstances. We were arguing. I felt the old tensions rise, as if the water were not on fire and full of death.

"You were taking Mitsy and Sadako away."

"Hart," he said, "they wanted to go."

Sunshine and Shadow
1946

Now, with the closed sign on the chandlery door and the logbook open to the final scribbled entry and the water blinking silver and blue whenever I glance out at Roebuck Bay, I find myself thinking about the day I stopped recording and started waiting. Scribbles. Black words scratched onto white paper. Only memory can create the sunshine and shadow that surround them.

On March 4, 1942, I wrote: *We fear invasion.* In fact, for days after the air raid we lived on a knife-edge, misinterpreting every sign. We saw another spotter plane — but it was only the Reverend Poole in his flimsy Desoutter, come to pray over us and soothe a few souls. *Smoke out at sea — an invasion fleet?* But it was only a coastal steamer.

An evacuation of the town was swiftly arranged. A construction company working at the airfield provided trucks and a few of us provided cars, and we set out in convoy, south into the desert.

But the elements defeated us.

In a sense, we were storm-tossed creatures. It was a season of storms, if sieges, land battles, and aerial bombardments are reckoned along with torrential rain and the lash and mutter of changeable winds.

My records show that the Wet of 1942 dumped twenty-eight inches of rain on the West Kimberley coast in just six weeks. Many of the roads were washed away or impassable for days at a time. A chain of muddy lakes appeared along the coastline between Broome and Port Hedland, and tens of thousands of frogs. For days we'd been dodging frogs, treading on them, waking and going to bed with them. The skin of the earth seemed to crawl, tormented by their tiny pads. We sleepwalked through the enervating hours of daylight, and slapped away the mosquitoes and sandflies that multiplied in ponds and cast-off car tires to swarm over us at night. Livestock drowned on the stations. Water seeped into the air-raid shelter as quickly as we could pump it out. Whenever someone such as the Reverend Poole landed at the town, he'd skim the treetops first, gauging the floodline on the airstrip, then splash down, skip and skitter toward the leeward side of the hangar, and lash his little airplane to the ground. There is always a gusting wind at that time of the year. The good Reverend's little plane would tremble like a leaf.

And so our evacuation convoy was forced to turn back. We were gone for only two days. After that, we tended to leave at dawn and head for the scrub, wait there for a few hours, then return to our homes. An afternoon raid from the air seemed unlikely. The Japanese base was on Timor, which would mean the pilots would be making the return trip in darkness if they attacked in the afternoon.

There were, in fact, three more raids on Broome — one in late March and two in August. They were reminders, really, for very little damage was done. But Broome was pretty much a dead town then anyway, compared to those two weeks when so many Dutch colonialists streamed through and planes jostled for space on the land and the water.

These days I manage the chandlery and look after my father. He's regained most of his speech and mobility, but spends much of his time as a kind of historian of the war, filling scrapbooks with newspaper clippings and reading every book he can that might help him "understand the Jap mind."

Alice was just skin and bone when the Americans found her, with other nurses and some civilian women and children, in a dust and bamboo-hut compound on Sumatra. Many of her teeth had fallen out and tropical ulcers had left craters in her legs and her eyes were wide and ravaged-looking in a pinched face. And that was how *we* found her, despite weeks of attention by Army doctors, who'd tried to fatten her up so that we at home would not be too horrified by her.

She says little about her long years away. She'd been picked up by a Chinese fisherman on Penang when the hospital ship sank, and had made her way to Singapore, where she worked in one of the hospitals, patching up the wounded who were coming through from Malaya. She'd written to tell us that she was safe and well, but that letter didn't arrive until weeks after my father's stroke, weeks after the Broome raid. It was false comfort to us by then. We didn't know if she'd escaped from Singapore before February 15 or been imprisoned there. In fact, she'd been evacuated hours before the surrender, but got only as far as Sumatra in a little boat with other nurses and a handful of wounded soldiers. Less than a month later, the Japanese had captured her.

She stayed with us for a year when she got back, then went south to Hobart. She wants, she says, to live where there is no hint of the tropics. She intends to go to London one day, to meet Ida's family.

I didn't see much of Jamie after pulling him from the water. He'd seen something in my eyes that had made him afraid and that I wish I'd never revealed, or even felt. He was posted to Darwin some time later, then New Guinea, where he was killed. He almost made it through. Just a few days before the war ended in the Pacific, his Hudson lost power on takeoff and plowed into a stand of coconut palms at the end of a log landing strip in a mountain valley.

You could say that Mitsy and I enjoy a kind of friendship now. We'd started off as friends, were lovers for a while, and then there was hate and indifference. Now friendship has replaced all of that, but a friendship that can't offer or ask too much.

When the smoke had cleared and there were no more bodies to be pulled from the water, she'd said to me, "Hart, will you take us to the jail? Please?"

It was the only safe place for Mitsy and her mother. She knew that. According to the final entry in my logbook Jamie flew them south the next day, where they were put on a train to Adelaide, and then taken to the internment camp for the Japanese at Tatura, in Victoria.

Mitsy made the first move. Three years ago a letter came from her. It was marked *Passed by the Censor,* but there was nothing in it to concern a censor in the first place: no secrets, nothing to undermine the war effort.

Dear Hart, she wrote:

I've been thinking about you such a lot, wondering whether or not to write. My mother, wise soul, said, "Daughter, write."

I should start by saying that I'm sorry we didn't tell you what our intentions were. When you found us with Jamie that day, it must have looked deceitful. But Hart, we were so miserable. In the end I had to ask Jamie to be our go-between with his father. A camp was the best place for us.

You won't blame Jamie, will you? Yes, he loved me, but our meeting each other had nothing to do with that and everything to do with negotiating our internment. In fact, I told him that it was you *I loved. What I didn't tell him was that I was waiting for you to feel better about me.*

We're well. We're treated kindly. My mother has found two women from her province in Japan. Me? I'm writing to you, aren't I?

Three long years, hundreds of letters. But the waiting will be over soon. The authorities have begun to release the internees. Last week it was Joe Suzuki, and as he stepped onto the jetty carrying all of his possessions in a duffel bag, the locals shouted at him, just as they will shout at Mitsy. It won't be easy. We may not make it.

This book was designed by Elizabeth B. Parisi.

The art for the jacket was created by Kim McGillivray,

using photography and digital art.

The text was set in Adobe Garamond,

a typeface designed in 1929 by Frederic W. Goudy.

The display faces were set in CG Coronet and Futura.

The book was printed on 50-pound Renew Antique paper

and bound at R.R. Donnelley & Sons

in Crawfordsville, Indiana.

Manufacturing was supervised by Jeanne Hutter.